# The Breakout

## NIKKI JEWELL

This one is for all the amazing book friends I've met along the way. The road to becoming an author is not an easy one, but it's a hundred percent worth it to get to know you all. Stories unite us like no other medium, and there's always room for a little more love in this world.

Be a good girl and read a book.

1.THE HEAT – THE SCORE
2.LIVIN' FOR THE WEEKEND – FITZ AND THE TANTRUMS
3.ANOTHER LEVEL – OH THE LARCENY
4.REAL GOOD LIFE – THE MOWGLI'S
5.WHAT WE LIVE FOR – AMERICAN AUTHORS
6.LOST BOYS – OCEAN PARK STANDOFF
7.ANIMAL – THE NEON TREES
8.KALEIDOSCOPE – A GREAT BIG WORLD
9.SUNRISE – HIGH DIVE HEART
10. RECKLESS – JAXSON GAMBLE
11. WRITTEN IN THE WATER – GIN WIGMORE
12. CALIFORNIA – SILENT PILOT
13. MY TYPE – SAINT MOTEL
14. SOMEONE ELSE – DYLAN
15. GOOD TIME – OCEAN PARK STANDOFF
16. BEST FRIEND BREAKUP – LAUREN SPENCER SMITH
17. CELEBRATE THE RECKLESS – MAGIC GIANT
18. PRETTY GIRL – LAPEER
19. BRING IT ON HOME – AMERICAN AUTHORS
20. HIGH – STEPHEN SANCHEZ

# Chapter One

## Jordan

My heart picks up speed at the cheery tinkle of the doorbell as my last customer of day exits. The way she's clutching the book to her chest lets me know I've found a kindred soul, and she'll probably be back for the next one in the series. Nothing gives me quite the high of helping someone find their new favorite author. I'm especially buzzed about this one since I'll get to meet her in person this weekend at Romancing the Windy City. The big romance book con is only a little over a four-hour drive, but I've never been able to attend thanks to school, work, my mother.

The surface of the paperback is smooth under my fingertips as I hug it to my chest. I place it down with care on top of the pyramid of Melanie Arbour books. Aspen might make fun of my vampire and fairy smut addiction, but he doesn't really mean it. In fact, I'm convinced he's a secret romance fan. I slip my phone out of my pocket for like the millionth time, glancing at the door, but it refuses to reward me. She better get here on time.

My best friend won't care if I miss his game, but I promised I'd be there. He probably pledged a life debt to his coach to get the time off practice to drive me to the conference. Letting him down never gets any easier. I hate when she does this to me.

"Aw c'mon, Fitz!" I scold the furry little fiend as he twists his lithe black body around my feet, tripping me up. His antics have me dropping an armload of thin books as I'm trying to make my way to the children's nook at the back to stock up.

The delicate triangle of his whiskered face peers up at me with the most cattish of unconcern. His sleek hair is smooth under my fingers as I run them down his back a few times. I'm a sucker for our little bookstore cat. He wandered into the store three years ago, and after a week of putting him outside every day, we granted him permanent resident status. Every bookstore needs a cat, after all.

The bell tinkles behind me again. Finally. I push myself out of my crouch, spinning around. A tight knot forms in my chest at the apologetic look on my mother's face. Her slim fitting black slacks and the soft ivory sweater hugging her torso would have been enough to give her away without the guilty look on her face.

I shake my head. "No, Mom. I have to go to Aspen's game."

"Sweetie, that boy has so many hockey games, it's ridiculous. And you go to all of them."

I bite my lip to avoid shooting down her exaggeration. I can't cheer him on at nearly as many games as I'd like to, thanks to this exact problem. "Yeah, he's my best friend, and I promised I'd go. He did, after all, get special permission to take a few days off training to join me at the convention."

Her shiny white teeth contrast with the crimson lipstick she's replaced her usual subtle pink gloss with. I'll never understand why she feels the need to change her entire personality whenever some guy asks her out. No wonder her relationships never work. The guys she dates have no idea who she really is. Although maybe that's because she doesn't know either.

"Exactly. You're going to be spending the next few days with him. You can miss this game. Glenn is perfect." She looks like the personification of a heart eye emoji right now, talking about the latest in the string of men she thinks is going to change her life.

"That's what you said about the last one." And the one before, and the one before that. Ever since my father left her broken-hearted, she's been chasing love as if it's one of those rabbit things that greyhounds try to catch. It ends the same way for them. Eternal disappointment.

"Oh, but Glenn. He's a lawyer, and he's a partner at Devine & Hart." As if I'm supposed to know what that means. She laughs at the confusion on my face. "It's a big firm in the city. He's taking me to Botanique." She name-drops the super swanky restaurant in Detroit as if she goes there every day. "Can you pretty please close up the store tonight?" She presses her palms together in front of her mouth in a plea she knows I won't be able to resist.

Aspen will forgive me. He always does. A warm sensation spreads through my chest, in spite of the prickle of guilt rearing its head at the thought of my best friend. I'll send him a good luck text.

"Fine."

"Thank you so much, sweetie." There's a fresh bounce in her step as she closes the distance between us to give me a hug.

"Of course, Mom." Her hair falls over my shoulder in a smooth red waterfall. It's the opposite of the usual chaotic curls she shares with me.

She's off in a cloud of expensive-smelling perfume as I'm bent over picking up the rainbow of children's books scattered across the carpet. The merry little bell signaling her departure doesn't have quite the same charm as before.

# Chapter Two

## Aspen

Jackson's exuberant back slap sends me hurtling through the front door. The air is stifling with the heat of the random bodies already crowding our place. It's always like this on nights we get the win. Everybody wants a piece of the star hockey players. Hell, even when we lose, they come out in droves, offering their condolences, while drinking our beer.

The guys are lapping it up. Jax's usual sunny smile has that extra quirk at the corner that lets me know he's off to charm some chick into his bed as he charges past me. He runs a hand through the sunshine-streaked hair he took the time to dry and style before we left the arena. Vain bastard needs to be taken down a notch, but I have a feeling the hurricane force of his charm is going to sweep someone off their feet tonight.

"Blond in the corner with the pink shirt is mine." He nods toward a girl with cleavage straining her tank top and a feral gleam in her eyes.

"All yours. Good luck." He's going to need it. For reasons I will never understand, he always goes for the ones who don't mind a challenge. He's only ever in it for the night and he's not shy about letting girls know it, but they all seem to think they can catch him. Maybe it's the California golden boy good looks. Deceptive on every level. He's not even from the golden state.

"Are you planning on having a little fun tonight?" He cocks his head. "Lots of pretty ladies here."

"Nah, man. Not tonight. Early morning." Not to mention I haven't been feeling it since I broke up with Natalie a couple of months ago. Not that I'm super broken up about it. We had fun, but it was always meant to be a casual thing.

"Right. You've got that book thing with Jordan, right?"

I nod, scanning the room for her fiery red curls. I was hoping she'd show up for the after party even though she couldn't make the game. Her mom has her running the store again. I know she loves it, but I also know her mom takes advantage of her. She never complains. But when you've known someone as long as we've known each other, you recognize the signs. I've probably got enough resentment simmering inside for the both of us.

"You two need to do the nasty and get it over with."

A snort escapes me. "Jordan and I? You need to get over that one. She's my best friend. I've known her since she still wore her hair in pigtails. She's like a sister." Those red braids come to mind, and an image of what she'd look like with them now pops into my head in a most unbrotherly way. I try to be discreet when I adjust myself in my pants, but Jackson catches the motion with a laugh.

"Sure, dude. Keep telling yourself that." I don't trust the smirk that twists up the corner of his mouth. "Wait. So, if you're not into her like that, mind if I have a crack?"

There's a roaring in my ears and my fist is flying out before I can stop it. "Don't you fucking dare."

Jackson clutches his shoulder. "Shit man, that hurt. I was only messing with ya."

My head knows that, but apparently I've got some hidden caveman instincts I never knew about. I take a few deep breaths to ease up the desire to punch him again.

He backs away with his hands thrown up in surrender. "Well, have fun. I will not be seeing you in the morning if all goes well."

He pushes off on a direct line to the hot blond he was eyeing. Some poor freshman makes the mistake of getting in the way of Jax's prize. I laugh as the dude gets a solid hip check that sends him stumbling back for his impertinence.

My mood sinks further after I scan the room one more time and don't spot her. I have to run the gauntlet of congratulations and back slaps to get to the stairs. Normally I wouldn't mind, but tonight an exhausting mix of disappointment and excitement is weighing my limbs down. I'm looking forward to crashing for the night.

Something snags my attention, and I make one detour before heading up the stairs.

"Hey, man. How's it going?" My approach is slow and cautious, not knowing what kind of reaction I'm going to trigger.

The sight of the jagged red scar trailing down his cheek still sends a brief shock through my gut. Sebastian gives me a dark look over the shoulder of the brunette perched on his non injured leg. "How does it look like it's going?" His arm flexes as he tightens his hold around her waist, and she giggles.

"Listen. If you need anything..."

"I don't." He cuts me off, leaning in to plant his lips on the girl's mouth in a clear dismissal. He hasn't been the same since his injury and I wish I could help him out, but he's not ready yet. What he really needs is to get back on the ice, but that's not going to be possible for a while.

I ghost away toward the stairs. We're in for a long drive tomorrow and my bed is calling to me.

# Chapter Three

## Jordan

"You should definitely come to my talk at three. Us redheads need to stick together." I'm trying desperately to maintain some semblance of chill at the invitation from one of my absolute favorite authors of all time.

"Of course! Kellian couldn't drag me away from it."

A genuine smile lights up her face at the mention of the MMC from her latest series. "I doubt that."

"You're right. He could drag me away from my own wedding and carry me off on his horse." Fiddling with the dagger charm on my necklace, I pause while mustering the courage to ask. "And you think we can arrange that talk at Top Shelf?" The question bubbles out in a jumbled rush. It would be freaking amazing if I could get her to come to our little bookstore. She's the type of author that people camp out to see at big chain bookstores.

"For sure. I love supporting local bookstores." She scribbles something on the back of a card before slipping it to me. "My personal email. Most of these events go through my PA, but you can contact me direct. I don't want you getting lost in the crowd."

I feel like I'm about to drift up into the rafters as I float my way back to where Aspen is leaning against a wooden beam off to the side of the conference floor. He's trying to stay out of the swarm of bookish fans, but there's still a handful of girls closing in on him. I don't blame them. Eighty percent of the conference attendees are female, and he looks like he could have come right off the pages of one of their fave books. His dark hair and chiseled jaw scream book boyfriend. And that black Henley clinging to his muscled chest isn't helping matters. They probably think he's a cover model or something.

"Aspen, there you are." I run at him. There's zero doubt in my mind that he'll catch me when I fling my arms around him and leap.

As usual, he doesn't disappoint, letting out a startled laugh even as his hands clamp on my thighs to hold me steady. His fan club scatters. Mission accomplished.

"Thanks." Hot breath tickles my neck as he leans in, whispering the word into my ear.

"Anytime." A tingle of awareness sends an unexpected buzz through my nether regions. I pull in a sharp inhale, releasing my legs from around his waist. He doesn't let go right away, so I'm stuck hanging there for a moment as he gazes down at me through hooded eyes. I follow the movement of his tongue when it darts out to swipe at his full lower lip. Giggles from my left pull me out of my trance and I let myself slide. What feels like every muscle in his athlete's body scrapes against my sensitive skin on the way down.

I don't know if it's the high from meeting my favorite author. Maybe it's the change of venue, away from home and all the baggage that comes with it, but I'm hyper aware of his body inches from mine. I find myself wanting to lean in and taste his lips for the first time.

"How did that go?" His voice has gone a bit husky, but his question pulls me out of the moment.

It takes my scattered brain a second to clear the haze away. "Oh my god! It was amazing!!!" I'm jumping up and down at this point, but he's used to my explosions of joy. "She's going to come to Top Shelf for a signing. And," I check to make sure no one is listening in, dropping my voice low even though the general buzz of sound in the crowded space makes it unlikely anyone will overhear, "she gave me her personal email address."

"That's fantastic. That'll be amazing for the store."

"Right? We totally need this." I pull out my phone to enter her number into my contacts in case I lose the card. My face falls at the notification that pops up at the top of my screen. The storm of the century that my news notifications have been threatening us with for the past few days is apparently about to unleash on us early. All the warnings are to cancel any travel plans. We need to get back. I swing my phone around to show him.

"Maybe we should leave now." I can't stop my gaze from straying back toward Melanie's booth. She's still signing books for her adoring fans.

"No way. She's doing a reading at three, right? I'd never forgive myself if you missed that." A soft, relaxed smile curves his lips up as if he's totally unconcerned about the storm warning.

"App says the driving is going to get really bad, and you have to get back for practice, right?"

"Yeah, but I can drive in anything. It'll be fine. This is important to you. I'd never forgive myself if you missed it."

# Chapter Four

## Aspen

I t's not fine. My hands are gripping the steering wheel so tight my knuckles are white and aching, and there's a pit of fear in my gut I've never felt while driving. I love driving and I grew up in Michigan. I'm used to trekking through whatever shit the season has in store for us. This is something else, though. The snow started before we left the conference, but it's only gotten worse. The headlights are struggling to cut through the wall of white that greets me out the front windshield.

Jordan's excited chatter didn't stop for the first hour, but her huge smile has thinned to a grim line, and concerned wrinkles have popped up between her brows.

"I think we should stop, Aspen."

It's not the first time she's said the words, but I can't deny it any longer. After all, her life is in my hands. I would never forgive myself if I got into an accident and she got injured, or worse. The worse is unthinkable.

"Yeah. Can you look up a hotel or somewhere nearby we can stop?"

"I've got no cell service, but I'll keep my eyes open." I don't know how she can see anything out the window, but hopefully something gets through.

I have to slow to a crawl and there's no sign of anything for another tense half hour. Finally, a sign pops up. We're passing through some small town I've never heard of before.

"How about here? There's got to be somewhere to stay here."

My heart races as the wheels spin out on the slick surface. I drive into a skid, fighting to keep the tires on the road when I make the turnoff. It is not promising. I can only catch sight of the signs for various farms at the end of sweeping driveways. It's one of those middle of nowhere towns that's probably home to ten times as many cows as people. A tiny old bank sits on the corner of what looks like the main street, but there's no sign of a motel. I'm almost ready to turn up a random driveway to beg for shelter from a hopefully non murderous local when something catches my eye.

"A bed-and-breakfast!" Jordan claps her hands and I breathe my first easy breath since the roads turned treacherous.

# CHAPTER FIVE

## JORDAN

This place looks like it belongs in a small-town romance novel, or one of my fave cheesy Christmas movies. Its facade is white, with matching dormer windows on either side trimmed with gingerbread. No one has cleared the driveway, but there are a few snowy car shaped hills beside the more modern detached garage, and the lit-up windows are beckoning us in.

"I hope they have a room for us." I turn to Aspen while I'm pulling on the pink crocheted mitts and matching hat his mom handmade for me.

His lower lip pushes out in a pout, and he blinks at me with mossy green eyes. "How could they turn us away? Come on, give me your best lost puppy eyes."

"Dork." He breaks out into laughter as I shove him.

"But you love me????" His lips twist into my favorite crooked grin, but the warming tingle that spreads through me is sending up alarm bells. Danger. Best friend alert. Do not pass go. Do not catch feelings.

"Of course. Always." My voice drops to a whisper as I get caught up in his smile. My traitor brain slips back to that moment we had in the conference center. If there hadn't been a crowd of rabid book lovers nearby, I might have done something that would not have been good for our friendship or my future sanity. "Come on."

It's a bit of a struggle, but I force the door open and am immediately accosted by a gust of wind threatening to steal my breath. I can barely see two feet in front of me and the air is that kind of cold that wants to cause permanent damage to your fingers. I'm extra thankful we found a place to seek refuge. You hear horror stories sometimes of people who get lost and freeze to death in their cars. A different shiver runs up my spine at that nightmare scenario.

I sink up to my knees in the snow with each step, but I manage to stay on my feet until I hit a drift that sucks me down to my thighs. I'm struggling to extricate myself when Aspen's hands close over my waist and he lifts me up with ease. My knight in shining blue parka.

Beads of sweat are dripping into my eyes as I grab the pewter ring of the door knocker. It's hanging from the mouth of a friendly-looking gargoyle that I almost expect to come to life and ask for a password. Signs you read too many fantasy books. Check.

The cheery red front door opens before I've even finished my swing and I stumble into the front hall as my mitt gets tangled in the door knocker.

"Oh, I'm so sorry, my dear."

I free myself from the mitt to look up at our host. She belongs in the same fairy tale her adorable house and magical door knocker came from. Tight white curls surround rosy cheeks. Round gold frames perch on her slightly hooked nose in front of faded blue eyes that crinkle at the corners. Not to mention the ruffled flowery apron tied around her trim waist. She could be the kindly old grandmother in the story, or she could be the witch about to cook us in her giant cauldron. Could go either way. Hoping for the former.

"Hello. I'm Aspen, and this is Jordan." He casually slings his arm around my shoulder as he says my name. "Did you have a couple of rooms available?"

"Oh dears. Did you get caught in this awful storm? Come in. Come in."

She waves her hands at us, backing away from the front door to let us pass. I'm so tired by this point, I don't even care if she's planning on baking us in her next batch of cookies.

"Welcome to the Knotty Pine. I'm Norma. Let me take your coats for you."

Aspen glances back over his shoulder at his car. A generous layer of snow is already piling up on it like fluffy white frosting. "If you have rooms for us, I'll grab our bags."

"Of course. Go ahead. I'll just take your lovely girlfriend by the fireplace to warm up." Maybe she's planning on roasting me on a spit in her giant open fireplace.

I take a step back to go help Aspen, but he waves me off. "I got this. You go on and get warm." The door shuts behind him, cutting off the wind that was bringing in gusts of swirling snow.

After I surrender my coat to our host, she hangs it up, and I follow her down the hall. The wallpaper suits the vibe of the place with flowers tangled through pink and white stripes.

The living room is adorable. True to her word, there's a stone fireplace with a roaring fire crackling away. The smoky smell takes me back to the days when I'd go camping with Aspen's family. All that's missing is the sticky sweet scent of toasty marshmallows over a campfire. No sign of a pot large enough to boil a human, so she might really be the grandmother of the story rather than the evil witch. She leads me to the puffy cream couch, also scattered with pink flowers. I sense a theme here.

It's the opposite wall that finally puts my mind at ease. Five built-in bookshelves stretch up to the ceiling. The rich dark wood contrasts with the rest of the floral grandmotherly decor, but they're jammed full of books. Stacks of faded naked hardcovers mingling with shiny new paperbacks warm me better than the open flames ever could. Anyone with that many books must be trustworthy.

"Your bookcases are beautiful."

A wistful look crosses the older lady's face. "My Walter built those for me."

"Is that your husband?" I glance around, expecting him to pop into the room.

"Was. He passed away. I run this place by myself now."

"Oh, I'm sorry." I never quite know the right words to say when a stranger bares their soul like that.

"It's ok. He's been gone for five years. You never get over it, but the hole gets smaller, easier to bear. I'm just glad we got sixty years together."

"Sixty? That's incredible." I'd love that kind of stability and permanence.

"Yes. We were friends from the time we were little kids running wild together. This place used to be a working farm, but we sold off most of the land twenty years ago and turned it into a bed-and-breakfast."

"It's lovely. Do you read a lot? I'm a huge bookworm, and my mom owns a bookstore."

"How marvelous. I love to read. Mostly romance now. If it doesn't have a good dirty sex scene, it's not my bag."

I can't prevent the snort that slips out at her words. That took an unexpected turn.

"What? An old lady can't enjoy a little smut? Feel free to browse my collection. The first bookcase is all my favorite reads." She bobs her wispy white brows at me and gives me a wink.

"No reason at all. I might check it out later. Hopefully, we won't have to stay too long. Aspen really needs to get back for training."

"He seems nice, your fella. Definitely a keeper."

"Oh.... Aspen isn't my boyfriend. We're just friends. We've known each other forever."

"If you say so."

I'm about to lodge a further protest when the object of our conversation enters the room. He drops our bags with a dramatic groan, whipping his wool hat off. His sandy brown hair is buzzed short at the sides, but the top is damp with sweat and sticking up in wild spikes all over his head that have me itching to smooth them down.

# Chapter Six

## Aspen

Our light weekend bags are a breeze, but I groan and make a big show of putting them down, knowing it'll bring a smile to my favorite person's face. The two ladies are huddled together on a couch so ugly it almost looks nice. Nah, it's hideous. I'm going to have nightmares about giant, murderous flowers chasing me through the snow. But it suits our grandmotherly host.

"What's up ladies?"

Norma rises to her feet with a grace I wouldn't expect of someone her age. "Let me hang up your coat for you, dearie."

"Nah. Thank you so much, but I can hang it up if you show me where." My mother would be ashamed of me if I made this sweet old lady do extra work that I'm perfectly capable of.

Norma advances on me with a determined look on her face as I'm unzipping my thick winter coat. "Nonsense.

I've got this." She slides her hands over my shoulders to help me off with my coat, giving my biceps a squeeze. My shoulders relax after she lifts the thick jacket off, so I can't be too mad about it.

"Oh yes, Jordan. You definitely need to keep this one."

She's off in a flash back down the hall I came from, leaving me standing with my mouth gaping open.

"Did I imagine that?"

The musical tinkling of Jordan's laugh bubbles out." Nope. She was for sure checking out your muscles. You better watch out or you're going to find yourself locked down with a new girlfriend before this trip is over."

"You think she'd give us a room for free if I put out?"

Her laugh edges toward hyena cackles and before long, she's wiping tears from her eyes. Mission accomplished. My day is not complete until I've made my best girl smile.

When Norma pops back in, I hustle over to the couch to sink down next to Jordan, leaning in to whisper in her ear. "You'll protect me from her, won't you?"

The small gasp she makes when my breath tickles her ear pleases me more than it should. "Of course. Always."

Norma's pale blue eyes size us up as she claps her hands together, sinking into another eyesore of a chair across from us. This one features tiny red and yellow flowers.

"Tell me about yourselves. You're not axe murderers, are you? I can't let you stay here if you're going to chop me into little bits in the middle of the night."

Jordan snorts, slapping a hand over her mouth.

"As long as you don't boil us in a cauldron on that fire of yours." I jerk my head at the crackling flames that are throwing off so much heat my back is a little damp already.

"Oh, you don't need my help with that. You're letting off more than enough steam on your own. What do you do with those muscles, anyway?"

My mouth drops open at the question, but Jordan, of course, jumps to my rescue. "He plays hockey. We go to Lakeview College. He's on the hockey team."

Norma bounces in her ugly chair. "I love hockey. Are you any good? Are you going to go pro? When you do, can you bring me a signed picture? It would be so great to rub it in Dorothy's face at Bridge. She thinks she's so special because her grandson is a doctor." Her nose crinkles up in disgust.

"That's the dream. And sure, I'll bring you a pic if I make it." Give her some incentive to keep us alive. Pink rises to our host's papery cheeks when I give her a smile and a wink.

Jordan smacks my shoulder. "Stop being so modest. He's amazing. He's definitely getting signed when he graduates."

"Well, you're going to make an amazing WAG. Spice the place up with that gorgeous red hair of yours. Those hockey wives are all too blond and shiny. You'll do."

"We're not together. I told you that before. Not gonna happen."

Jordan's words are sharp and final in a way that hurts more than it should. She's only stating the truth.

"We'll see about that. Come on. Let me show you to your room."

I grab our bags and we follow Norma down another hall that looks like a greenhouse threw up all over it and up a forest green carpeted staircase to the second floor.

We pass a few doors before she pulls out an actual physical key and opens one that has a big red heart with the number seven painted on it.

"Here you go. The Lover's Suite. It's the last room I have available. The couple who had to cancel ordered the whole romance package and everything, so you're welcome to partake. You can use the bath salts and bubbles in the jacuzzi tub as well."

A cozy space is revealed as the door swings open. The decor is still predominantly floral but a little less chaotic than the rest of the house. At least it's all coordinated in shades of blue. The thing that really catches my eye is the single large bed that dominates the space. One bed, of course.

# CHAPTER SEVEN

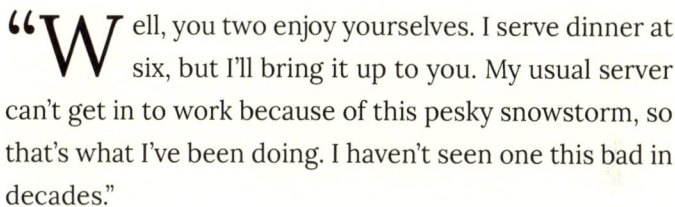

## JORDAN

"Well, you two enjoy yourselves. I serve dinner at six, but I'll bring it up to you. My usual server can't get in to work because of this pesky snowstorm, so that's what I've been doing. I haven't seen one this bad in decades."

Aspen takes a step toward our host. "You don't have to do that. I can come down and carry it upstairs for us."

She shakes her head, waving a hand at him. "Nonsense. I'm bringing it up for all the guests. Oh, you might want this." As she's backing out the door, she pulls a hand embroidered do-not-disturb sign off the inside handle and switches it to the outside. She throws in an exaggerated wink. Just in case we didn't get her point. "Don't worry, I'll knock before I bring dinner in."

My shoulders are once again shaking with giggles as the incorrigible old lady shuts the door, leaving us alone. My laughter dies down as that fact registers in my brain, and Aspen spins around to face me, rubbing the back of his neck.

"So, one bed?"

"I know, right? It's fine though. Look at it. It's huge. We can share. We'll pretend we're kids again. Right?" Right? My insides are already simmering at a low burn, thinking of that decidedly adult body sharing a bed with me. I'll go up in flames with the teensiest spark. Shit. I'm in trouble.

"Riiiight. Like we're kids again." His eyes drop to my chest and trail down my body, scorching a line wherever they touch.

I prowl the room, checking out every corner of the little blue space. I'm trying to keep my mind on anything but what's under those jeans. I mean, I've seen him shirtless in the summer at the pool, but what about the rest of him? Nope. Stuff that thought down and lock it up in the black box reserved for the darkest of fantasies. Do not think of your best friend like that. Your hockey playing best friend, no less. Sure, he's an amazing guy, but he's still going to become an NHL player and I know how that turns out. Hello. Dad. Not for me, thanks.

"Um. I'm gonna have a shower." Aspen, my normally confident bestie, is rubbing the back of his neck in a familiar gesture I've seen many a time when he's nervous. "That is, if you don't want to go first." Ever the gentleman.

"You go ahead." I wave him on.

He swings around, ducking into the bathroom as if there's a wolf on his heels and I'm left standing here all awkward like.

Enough. This is Aspen. We can totally do this. It's only going to be a day or two. A distraction. That's what I need. A bookshelf next to the window catches my eye. Painted forget-me-nots cascade down the sides of the white shelf.

I skim over the spines. From Blood and Ash. Nice. I love JLA. Romance, romance, and more romance. Fantasy, contemporary and everything in between. Norma certainly has her preference. Somehow, I don't think reading smut is going to help cool down the fire that's been burning in my core since I made the mistake of jumping on Aspen at the conference. Ugh. I finally spot a harmless-looking book I've never seen before. The artsy photograph of a woman on the cover screams women's fiction. Should be safe. I snatch it and jump up onto the cozy bed. It's a bit of a struggle and I fail my first attempt, sliding to the floor in a heap of awkwardness.

My tired body sinks into the fluffy mattress once I get up there and I settle back with my fingers curled around the paperback.

# CHAPTER EIGHT

## JORDAN

*H*is hands trail up her sides, sending shivers to her core...

"Whatcha reading?"

Aspen's voice slices through the unexpected smut so hard, I drop the book. Heat scorches up my neck to my cheeks until my entire body is on fire. Sometimes being a pale redhead is not cool. No secrets.

"Oh, it's like that, is it?" He chuckles.

I hide my face in my hands, but slide my fingers open a crack to peek at him. Are you shitting me??? He's wearing nothing but a pair of gray sweatpants clinging to his still damp hips as he towels himself off. My mouth gapes as I drink in the sight of his smooth skin stretched taut over the ripples of his abs.

He glances down. "What?"

His hands fly up to block the pillow that I aim at his head. "Are you kidding me?"

Hints of brown peek through the green of his eyes as they widen in faux shock, but the corner of his mouth twisting up into a smirk gives him away. He knows exactly what he's doing. "Really? Do you think that is helpful?" I wave a hand at all the bare skin, begging for my hands or better yet tongue to slide over it.

"I'm sorry. Didn't think it would bother you. Nothing you haven't seen before."

He's technically correct. We spend a fair amount of the long summer days in his backyard pool or at the lake. However, it's rather different seeing his skin on display in the bright sunshine of a summer day as opposed to now, here, alone in this room. There's an almost tangible electric crackle in the air. Not to mention... "Don't pretend you don't know." I shake my head at him.

"What are you talking about?"

"The gray sweatpants."

He glances down again, bursting into laughter. "I just grabbed them out of my bag. I wasn't thinking. Sorry. Is it too much for you? Want me to change?"

He stalks toward me, leaning over the bed to get up in my face and lifting a brow. "Too hot for you to handle?"

Every inch he gets closer pushes another logical thought out of my brain until I'm nothing but a collection of overheated hormones and erratically sparking synapses. The smile drops off his lips and they part as we gravitate toward each other.

Loud knocking jolts me out of my lust filled haze, sending me flying back.

"Dinner is here, dearies. I hope I'm not interrupting anything."

A nervous giggle escapes me as Aspen grabs his discarded shirt, shoving it on before he answers the door.

"I can grab that." His deep voice rumbles out with a nervous edge to it.

"Nonsense. I'll bring it in and put it down on the desk."

She peers over her round lenses at me sitting on the bed with my knees pulled up under my chin and a face that probably rivals my hair in the color department.

Aspen stands behind her, shifting from one foot to the other, arms crossed over his wide chest, as she fusses with the tray she brought up to our room. I'm surprised the tiny old woman got it up here. It's a solid-looking pine tray overflowing with silver domes, small plates, and glasses. I'm tired just thinking of dragging it up the stairs.

After what feels like about a century, she straightens up, brushing her hands together and heading for the door.

"You can leave that tray outside the door when you're finished. Oh, and help yourself to those chocolate-covered strawberries. They're only going to go bad if you don't eat them. Food of love, you know."

I giggle again as she walks out with a last wink over her shoulder. She's a big winker that one. My giggle turns into a full-blown cackle when Aspen turns around to lock the door behind her, and I notice the tag sticking out the back of his shirt.

"Umm, you might want to fix your shirt there, dude." Dude. That's a safe word to use to dampen the sexual tension that's been running rampant through the tiny room since we stepped in. I'm not sure what exactly has changed. I've always been aware of Aspen and his hotness factor, but something about this time away from home has shifted my lust into overdrive.

"What?" He swings around with a quirked brow. Yup, he noticed how awkward that sounded. I never call him dude.

"You put your shirt on inside out, and I have no doubt in my mind that our lovely host noticed. She's had her eyes all over you since we got here."

He looks down with a grimace, reaching a hand behind his neck to whip the shirt off in a single smooth move, revealing those abs all over again. Well, there goes the dude barrier. Side note. Why is it so hot when a guy takes his shirt off with one hand like that?

I can't quite tear my eyes away from his torso until the Lakeview tee slips back down in place, logo side up this time.

# Chapter Nine

## Aspen

Her heated gaze sticks to me like glue the entire time I fix my shirt. It has my dick jumping in the gray sweats I may have grabbed on purpose, contrary to what I told her. I don't know what I'm expecting to happen, but ever since she jumped on me to save me from those ravenous book girls, I've been fighting a hard on. The white-knuckle drive in the snowstorm dampened the lust temporarily, but it's come roaring back to life now that we're here in this room. Alone. With one bed.

I'm dying to touch her, but that would be a terrible idea, right? She's my best friend, and I'm not what she wants. She doesn't want some asshole hockey player. She saw more than enough of that lifestyle when her cheater of a dad was still around. Not that I'd ever treat her that way, but I get it. My cock, however, does not get the message. He really wants to see what's under that fluffy sweater that matches her eyes. The loose neck has slipped down one shoulder, revealing a scattering of kissable freckles. I deserve a trophy for not acting on these feelings for so many years. Fuck. How is it that I can't keep them in check now?

"I'll get it." I tell her as she slides her long legs in front of her.

There's only one small wooden chair at the light pine desk, so I bring the entire tray over, plopping it down on the bed and settling next to her. My knee brushes against hers when I cross my legs and it's enough to send another bolt of lust through me as if I'm still a teenager. Get yourself together.

I pull off a silver dome with a bow and a goofy flourish to distract myself, and my stomach growls at the garlicky goodness floating out. Cheese oozes out the sides of the generous helpings of lasagna sitting on white plates. Surprisingly, no florals. Creamy Caesar salad sprinkled with chunks of real bacon lends the illusion of a healthy side. I'll play along. This doesn't exactly fit in with my nutrition plan, but what Coach doesn't know won't hurt him, or me, let's be honest. I'm not afraid of much, but gotta respect the coach.

Jordan grabs a fork, scooping in a heaping mouthful with a moan that sends a shock through my system. I want to be the one making her moan. Wait. Am I jealous of lasagna? That's messed up.

"Oh my god, thish ish amazing." Her eyes shutter with pleasure and it has the unfortunate effect of putting a picture in my head of what she'd look like while I was making her come.

I grab a bite and have to agree. Rich tomato sauce, garlic, perfectly seasoned beef, and gooey cheese hit the spot perfectly after the long ass day we've had.

After we've cleared our plates, I offer to take them downstairs. No need to make Norma do the extra work. Not to mention the walk will help clear my head.

When I get back to the room, Jordan is nowhere to be seen, but her horrendously off-key voice is belting out "Go Big or Go Home" over the steady stream of the shower. The sound of her singing always makes me smile, no matter how awful she is. It's the complete commitment and joy she puts into the words that do it for me. Nothing makes me happier than when she's got a smile on her face.

A picture flashes into my mind of her in the shower, naked, water streaming down all her curves. That bright red bikini of hers has given me a pretty good idea of what she looks like. Just a few key pieces are missing, but my imagination runs wild thinking of those missing pieces. Her breasts are full and luscious. I can only imagine how her nipples would look like standing at attention, ready for my mouth and tongue to tease.

My eyes drift shut as I picture long red curls plastered to her body. In my head, her hands slide over every inch of her flawless skin. I'm barely aware of what I'm doing as my hand finds its way under the infamous sweatpants to my painfully hard cock.

A familiar tingle awakens at the base of my back as I stroke my hardness with urgent tugs. The Jordan in my mind has her hand between her legs parting her pink lips to circle her clit.

"Aspen!" Jordan's voice has me yanking my hands out of my pants to the disappointment of my aching dick. He doesn't realize how idiotic that idea was.

"What's up?" I clear my throat in a lame attempt to get rid of the huskiness.

"Can you grab the gel out of my bag?"

Gel? Sure. I got this. "Yeah."

I slide off the bed, jerking my waistband a little higher with a smirk. She's jammed her royal blue rolling suitcase with way too much stuff for what was supposed to be a two-night stay in Chicago. We did end up stuck here for an extra night or two, so maybe she was onto something. The bag gapes open as I ease the pressure on the poor zipper and my body shakes with laughter. The thing is half full of books. Books she brought with her, books she bought at the event. Fantasy, contemporary. All romance. No wonder that thing felt like I was carrying a bag full of rocks through the snow. I'm surprised I didn't disappear under a drift, never to be seen again. What would she miss more? Me or the books?

As I'm rifling through the non-books side of the bag, my groin heats all over again when I pull out the sexiest red lace bra. An image of her full, creamy tits encased in the see-through strappy number almost has me coming in my pants. C'mon. Give me a break here.

My fingers brush the smooth curved side of the bottle of gel she uses to tame her sexy-as -hell curls, and I rush it to the bathroom. I stick the bottle through the crack in the door being careful not to widen the gap.

"Thanks," she calls out through the misty heat that does shit to cool me down. Her damp fingers brush against mine as she grabs the bottle. Here's hoping she's clueless about the explicit thoughts that her luggage had racing through my head in spite of my best efforts. Who am I kidding? I didn't do much to fight them off.

# Chapter Ten

## Aspen

"**O**h my god. Give it back!"

Jordan's angry green eyes narrow to slits as she rips the stolen book from my fingers. She's adorably ridiculous with a t-shirt wrapped around her still damp curls, clutching the smutty book to her chest.

"What? I was bored. You were taking foreeever in there." Maybe I'm being a bit dramatic, but her hair care routine is pretty intense.

"That doesn't mean you get to steal my books. I haven't even read this one yet. Play on your phone or something like a normal person."

"If you wanted a normal person for a friend, then you shouldn't have punched out Ryan Turner in the first grade for making fun of our names. Sorry. Stuck with me now." I shrug and give her my best what-can-you-do face. That little shit busted my balls for having a "girl" name and Jordan the opposite. I'll never forget his shock when she made his nose bleed.

"You just love to bring that up, don't you? My dad got me in so much trouble." Her face falls at the mention of her dad, and an angry knot twists my stomach, wiping away the dark smirk at the memory.

That asshole isn't worthy of her tears, so I go for the distraction. "I was enjoying it. Stone was about to declare his undying love for Clarisse. Wait, no. That's not right. He was pounding her into the mattress he tied her to. Is that how you like it? Rough?" I bob my brows at her. Why did I say that? Now I'm picturing her sweet ass jiggling as I slam into her from behind, fingers digging into her lush hips.

"Seriously. What kind of question is that? You're literally the worst." It warms my insides to see the smile fighting to pull up the corners of her mouth. Mission accomplished.

"Ah, but you love me. Want me to read to you?" I make grabby hands at the book, but she pulls it out of reach.

"That's a signed copy. I don't want your dirty boy hands on it."

I hold my arms up in front of her. "These hands? These hands are immaculate."

"Nuh uh, I know where they've been."

"Are you trying to slut shame me?" My lower lip pushes out in a fake pout. "And with reading tastes like that? I would think you'd understand the importance of a healthy sex life."

"It's not all about the smut, you know. I love reading romance because..." Her eyes drift up to the ceiling and I love how she takes the time to consider her thoughts. "...real life is shitty enough. There are no guaranteed happy endings, but in books, especially romance books. Well, they're never going to let you down."

Pain shadows her face again, and I want to erase every single bad thing that's ever happened to her. Her dad leaving, her mom basically letting her be the adult. She deserves a happy ending.

"You know there are happy endings in real life. Look at my parents." The polar opposite of hers. They raised me and my six siblings with all the love they had to give. They sacrificed for us, though. Sacrifices I'm not willing to make. Dad could have played professional hockey. He was on his college team like me, and he was good. Real good. Just like me. Not bragging, it's a fact. I'm the captain of one of the best college hockey teams, and I'm going pro. Nothing is going to stop me. Not love, not family. Nothing.

A huge smile spreads across her freckled face. "Your parents are amazing, but I don't think they're exactly the norm." My crunchy, oddball parents are anything but normal. Normal is overrated.

"I dunno. There are billions of people on the planet. They can't be the only happily married ones." A wave of exhaustion has a massive yawn stretching my mouth, causing the last word to come out garbled.

"Maybe." The sad, cynical look that I hate has darkened her emerald eyes, dimming the usual passion that sparkles in them. "I think you need to go to sleep. Also, what happened to your shirt? Did you lose it?"

My eyes are already fluttering shut at her words. My last thought is of her mouth twitching with laughter as sleep pulls me under.

# Chapter Eleven

## Jordan

W arm rays of light drag me out of my blissful-
ly unconscious state. The smooth pillow shifts
rhythmically under my cheek, trying to lull me back into
dreamland. A familiar fresh and musky scent wraps me
in comfort. Wait. Skin? Where am I? Aspen. I squeeze my
eyes shut tighter as the realization hits that the pillow
barrier I erected to keep my wild hormones in check
failed miserably. I'm half on top of my best friend. Head
resting on the corded muscles of his shoulder, leg en-
twined with his, one hip resting dangerously close to his
hard dick. Yup. He's got morning wood and my lady parts
are dying to take full advantage of it.

At least he's still asleep, right? I crack my eyes the tee-
niest bit, lifting my head slowly so as not to wake him up
annnnnd find him staring back at me. There's not an iota
of his usual humor in those earthy eyes. They're hooded
and glazed over with lust. His lips part, and his tongue

darts out to slide between those lush lips, and that single motion snaps the last thread of my self-control. I can't resist. Nor can I remember all the reasons I should.

I lean in until we're so close we're sharing the same air and crash into him with the force of several years' worth of sexual tension. Calloused hands bite into my bare shoulders in a firm grip, jerking me in closer and hitting every alpha male fantasy I've ever had. Shivers ripple up my back as a hand slides up to tangle in my curls. They escaped their t-shirt prison sometime in the middle of the night.

The kiss is everything. Fireworks, shooting stars, every whisper of a touch sends bolts of heat to my core. His tongue sweeps into my mouth, tangling with mine in a fierce dance. I'm on fire, my nipples tingling as I press in closer. There are too many clothes between us. My skin is begging me to lose the thin barrier of my camisole so I can finally feel his beautiful heat pressed against my needy breasts.

The sweatpants are my biggest problem right now. Those need to go asap. His muscles contract as I slide my hands down his long torso, slipping my thumbs under the elastic blocking me from the rest of him.

His hips jerk up as my thumbs skate over those gorgeous distinctly male lines, pointing in the direction of the one thing I want more than anything. Probably ever.

I lean in, following when he pulls back with a groan. My lips seeking the warmth that's been rudely torn away.

His firm grip on my hair and shoulder has shifted to a gentle push. And as if I stepped out in the ice storm that's been pummeling the outside world, the raging inferno inside is snuffed out. I find myself straddling my best friend as he pushes me away.

"Jordan. We can't."

"Pretty sure we can." I feel the need to protest, even if the tingles are sputtering out.

"You're my best friend. We can't do this. We'll wreck everything."

He's sliding backward to sit up, and I resist the urge to reach out so I can pull him back under me. If he doesn't want this. If he doesn't want me, then there's nothing I can do to make him.

He reaches out a finger, sliding it under my chin to tilt my face up. "Hey. It's not that I don't want to. God... I would love nothing better than to sink inside you as deep as I can go...and... But we can't. You mean everything to me. I can't lose you."

I cock my head to the side, chin still resting between his thumb and finger. "So, what you're saying is, you want me?" I selectively pick those words out of the jumble that came out of his mouth.

"Yes. Hell, yes. But we shouldn't."

I nod and pull away. "Fine."

"Jordan. You're not mad at me, are you?"

"Nope." I pop the p, turning away.

He's right. We shouldn't. No matter how much we both want to. No matter how delicious those gray sweatpants look, clinging to his tight hockey butt and thickly muscled thighs. That's all it is. And being trapped in this hotel.

Maybe we can get out today. Get back to real life where I don't lust after my best friend nonstop. Only occasionally.

# Chapter Twelve

## Aspen

W e're not getting out of here today. No fucking way. We're used to snowstorms around here, but this is beyond anything I've seen in my lifetime.

I lean the borrowed shovel against the wall beside the front door. I came out to clear my head and check out the storm situation and ended up clearing the front walkway. Jokes on me. There's already a thin white dusting of snow covering my hard work. It felt good, though. Get a little exercise, burn off some of that pent up energy that's been building since we got here. Plus, I figured Norma could use the help.

I told Jordan it was to check things out, but honestly, I needed to cool the fuck down. And I couldn't have picked a better place for that. The world has gone white with the snow still barreling down from the sky. It's as if the weather is taunting me. You're trapped here. Stuck trying to resist the sweet curves of your best friend. Good luck.

I tilt my head up to the sky, letting every cold wet flake slap me in the face with a dose of reality. C'mon. I did the right thing. I could have let her peel these sweatpants down my legs and slide herself down on my cock, riding me like one of those heroines in her romance novels. My dick's already waking from his slumber at the thought of her wet heat encasing me.

But I didn't. I did the right thing. She wants a stable life here with her bookstore, and she deserves a guy who will be there for her every day. Someone she can count on for the first time in her life. And that can't be me. I love her, and she's always been the hottest woman I've ever seen, but I'm going pro. I already train, travel, and work out constantly, and this is only a college team. One of the best in the league, but it's only a fraction of what life will be like when I go pro. And as much as I love her, I'm not going to let anyone stand in the way of my hockey goals. No pun intended. Not like my dad did.

I'm doing it for both of us.

All my good intentions disappear under the weight of one word when I get back to the room. Jordan's standing with her back to me. The light coming through the window illuminates the gold glints hidden in her red hair as she looks out into the blizzard. It's my name on her back that's doing it for me. Seeing Ellory spelled out in bold white letters trips some sort of forgotten caveman instinct in me, telling me to lay my claim on her.

It's not even that I've never seen her wearing my jersey. She's been to plenty of my games over our lifetime of friendship. With seven kids, my parents were often too busy to stay and watch, but I knew she was always there in the stands. Maybe watching, maybe reading a book. But always there for me.

But she's not a kid anymore. The sight of that purple fabric draped over her rounded ass finally burns through the last frayed thread of my careful control. Heat tears through me like a flash fire, and I stride forward with one word running through my mind on repeat.

Mine.

# CHAPTER THIRTEEN

## JORDAN

I heard the key in the lock, but I exercised every ounce of self-control I had left to stay facing the window. A satisfied smile turns up the corner of my lips. I knew the jersey would do it. Wait until he finds out there's nothing underneath it.

I finally turn around when I hear his heavy footsteps eating up the ground. I barely catch the glaze of passion in his eyes before his hands close around my biceps. He yanks me into him, bending down to reach me.

He nips at my lower lip, tugging it between his teeth. Rough hands shift to my cheeks, sealing us together. I was already wet just thinking about what this was going to do to him. Now, I'm practically dripping.

Our mouths tussle for dominance until we're both panting. My lips tingle with need as he pulls away to rest his forehead on mine.

"What are we doing, Jordan?" The words come out in a growl.

Oh, no. He's not going to back out of this now. I won't let him. "We're enjoying each other's company." Maybe not as much as we could be. I'd be enjoying his company a hell of a lot more if he'd just lose the inhibitions and the clothes. Way too many clothes.

"But..."

His lips are soft against the finger I place over them to silence his doubts. I turn my head up, arching a brow in a dare. His eyes have darkened to the color of a shadowy corner of the woods. "No buts. What if... what if we let this be our Blue Castle? The place where we can let go and be whoever we want to be. When we go back home. Back to reality. Then we can go back to being friends."

He doesn't bat an eye at the reference to my favorite L.M. Montgomery book. Doubt is warring with need in his expression, but I can see the moment his 'we shouldn't' turns into a 'hell yes.' "Just for here?" The waver in his voice tells me everything I need to know.

I nod. "What happens at the Knotty Pine stays at the Knotty Pine." I stretch up on my tiptoes, sealing the promise with a kiss. A kiss that has my core unfurling with a need that vibrates throughout my entire body.

Strong hands clamp under my thighs, and he lifts me effortlessly into his arms. My legs wrap around his waist, and his hard length presses against my pussy, begging to be released from those GD sweatpants. That's how I know he wanted this. He never changed out of those freaking sweatpants. He knew exactly what they did to me, and he left them on.

My hands scrabble under his shirt to get at all that smooth skin underneath, and a shiver runs through him when I make contact. I'm still trying to yank off the damn thing when he pulls away with a smirk on his kiss-swollen lips.

The soft mattress gives under my weight as he tosses me onto it. He reaches a hand behind his back, losing the damn thing in seconds. My eyes drink in all the dips and ripples of his hard-earned muscles.

I'm dying to feel his flesh against mine, but he stills my hands when I grasp at the hem of his jersey.

"Leave it on. For now. Fuck, I like seeing you in my colors."

The jersey chafes at my nipples as he yanks me to the edge of the bed, dropping to his knees between my thighs. His eyes flick up to mine, and then... Fuck me. His tongue darts out in a slow slide up each thigh, not quite reaching that spot where I need him the most.

My fingers tangle in his messy hair with a plea for mercy. His rough fingers pinch a nipple with a sharp bite that has my hips bucking up.

"I'm in charge." Those words coming out of his mouth are everything.

Finally, finally, his mouth closes over my clit. His tongue and teeth tease as he licks and sucks at that spot that has need building in my core.

"You're so fucking wet." A thick finger slides up inside me with ease, as if to prove the point.

My head falls back as my body bows under the suction of his lips and the invasion of his thick digit. I slide my hands up under the jersey to toy with my nipples, swirling my fingers around the sensitive buds in time with his thrusts.

My legs are shaking as the pressure builds. The current sparks from my breasts to my groin and back again in a constant loop of pleasure beyond anything I've ever experienced.

It builds and builds until I don't think I can stand it anymore.

A second finger joins the first in a sharp thrust that sends me over the edge. "Aspen!" I scream his name as my body shudders so hard the world goes dark, falling back to the bed in a boneless panting heap.

My pussy clenches at the loss when he pulls out of me and I drag my eyes open in time to see him slide those fingers slick with my juice into his mouth, licking them clean.

"You taste fucking amazing. Now let's lose that jersey."

Cool air nips at my sensitive nipples as he drags it off. His sweatpants go next, leaving my mouth gaping. Holy shit. Like I knew he had a big package. I've seen the signs of it, but that thing's a beast.

# Chapter Fourteen

## Aspen

The wide eyes and open mouth tell me everything. She can admire it next time, though. Now I need to be inside her. Fuck, she's incredible. Her softly rounded curves, the light freckling across her shoulders. I want to discover and press a lingering kiss to every single one.

She's everything I've dreamed of and more. So much more. Getting to see her like this, to feel her soft skin under my hands, taste the sweetest pussy I've ever gotten my mouth on. Even if it's only for these brief moments, it'll be worth it. Worth the pain I know I'm going to feel when this is over. When I get my heart ripped out in a couple of days.

Her bright eyes follow my hand as it slides along my length in a few quick strokes before I slide a condom on. Thank fuck I had some in my travel bag.

The fiery red curls nestled above her pussy are inviting me in, and I shift her up the bed, admiring those gorgeous tits tipped in dusky pink nipples. I can't help ducking my head down to swipe my tongue over each one before I shift my hips over her, lining up with that oh so ready slit.

A groan escapes me as the head of my cock gets its first taste of her. I still at the gasp that slips from her mouth as the first couple of inches press in.

"It's ok. Keep going. Just holy fuck, you're big."

The smug grin turns into a shaky moan as I press in further. She grabs a handful of my ass and that's all the encouragement I need to plunge all the way to the hilt. I pull all the way out to slam right back into her again and again until the telltale tingle at the base of my back has me slowing down. She feels fucking amazing, and all I want to do is pound into her until I explode, but I hang on to the last thread of self-control I have to reach between us.

Her body jolts when my thumb makes contact, her eyes flying open again. "I can't."

"You can't what, Jordy?" The nickname slips out, but it feels right even in this moment.

Her gaze flicks down. "Come again."

"Oh, you can, and you will." My thumb is back on the magic button between her legs, swirling in a steady rhythm as I bend my head down to one of those beautiful tits. I almost lose it when I get that sweet flesh in my mouth. I alternate from one side to the other, continuing to plunge my length inside her until we're both vibrating.

And I can feel it. She's almost there. Her pants and gasps coming faster. Body glistening with sweat. I close my teeth on her right nipple with a sharp nip and she screams. Most beautiful fucking sound I've ever heard.

Her pussy pulses around my dick, grasping at me as I pump into her faster. And the tingle builds until I lose it. I roar my release into her clenching pussy. Holy fuck. Shaky arms threaten to give out on me. I blow out a deep breath and roll to my side, scooping an arm under her back to take her with me.

Post sex cuddling is usually not my thing, ok by usually I mean never, but I have zero desire to let her go. Ever. I pull her into my chest, dropping a kiss on the top of her head.

# Chapter Fifteen

## Jordan

Never have I ever hated the trill of my ringtone more. The obnoxious sound jerks me out of what may be the best dream I've ever had. I slap my hand on the table beside the bed to shut it up, knocking it to the floor with a soft thud. My brain is all sleep fuzzy, and it takes a moment to remember where I am when a heavy arm tightens around my waist.

I guess that wasn't the most incredible dream I've ever had. Nope. Just the most incredible sex I've ever had. Aspen. Who knew that goofy grin and floppy hair hid such raw need.

I get a brief respite from the ringing before it starts up again. I'm slapping my hands over my ears as it screams at me from its place on the floor.

My mouth stretches into a wide yawn, and I fluff up my out-of-control curls as I sit up. If you can't tame them, just own them is the philosophy I've learned from years of dealing with the disaster that is my hair. I didn't always feel that way. I used to despise my red hair with the passion of Anne Shirley.

"Ignore it." Aspen's gruff voice grumbles from behind me.

"Can't. It's probably my mom." She's the only one who actually calls me on the phone other than telemarketers, and they're never that persistent.

"Exactly." He's trying to hide his frustration, butthere's a subtle twitch at the corner of his right eye. After decades of friendship, I can read him way better than he'd like.

The hand I peel off my naked torso is so large it covers my entire abdomen. I finally drag it off so I can sit up and swing my legs over the side of the bed.

"Fuck." The curse comes out in a grumble behind me.

I twist around to catch Aspen staring at my ass with a sheen of admiration in his eyes. I follow the long, glorious path from his mossy eyes, past the sparse hairs on his chest, all the way to his thick length. It's already hard and responds to my admiring gaze with a twitch, ready to go for a round two we don't have time for. A twinge between my legs reminds me of what it felt like when it was stretching me wide. I'm almost ready to climb back on for a second ride when my phone lets out another insistent buzz.

I snatch the offending piece of metal off the floor, meandering to the bathroom and collecting the discarded jersey to drop over my head. I have zero desire to have this conversation in the buff.

"Hi, Mom." I try to keep my voice upbeat, but it comes out a little flat.

"Jordan. Where are you?" Her voice has that ragged edge that lets me know she's been crying. All the problems that floated away this weekend come crashing down, dragging me back to reality. The smooth cold surface grounds me as I let the heaviness in my body pull me down the side of the jacuzzi tub. This won't be the quick conversation I was hoping for.

"You know where I am. I sent you a text as soon as my cell service came back up. We're at a little inn waiting out the storm."

"I need you."

I tilt my eyes up, studying the brown swirls of water damage on the ceiling, a slow exhale slipping through my lips. "What's wrong, Mom?" I used to panic when I got calls like this, but they're all too familiar now. It can't be a genuine emergency. It never is.

"Glenn broke up with me." Her voice comes out broken like it does every time this happens.

"It'll be ok, Mom."

"Can't you come home? I don't think I can work at the store today."

"Mom, it's not safe to drive. Even in Aspen's SUV. We can't leave yet. Maybe tomorrow." I turn to the white wall of snow still swirling outside the window. Maybe. "Can't you call Clara to come in for a shift?"

"I tried, but she has an exam this afternoon. I told her she could study there, but she said no." I hear the implication behind her words. She thinks Clara is being selfish for putting school first.

"You've gotta go in then, Mom. We can't afford to lose a day of sales." When I'm not there to look after things, she tends to keep erratic hours. Sometimes closing the store early to go on one of her dates, sometimes not opening at all if she slides into one of her post break up depressions.

"Oh, don't be silly, it'll be fine." She dismisses my request with a careless lack of concern. "I don't think I can do it. I really liked him. I thought he was the one. Why do they always leave me like this?" There's a whine in her tremulous voice, and the seeds of a headache form at the base of my skill.

"It's not you, Mom. Listen. I'll be home as soon as I can get out of here safely. Please try to open the store, at least for a few hours." I'm sure my pleas are hitting a brick wall, but I have to try.

And now presenting the reason I can't wait to graduate next year. My mother. Once I'm finished, I can run Top Shelf full time, and then I can stop worrying that we're going to lose it. My legacy. The one good thing my father did before he abandoned us.

The only time I see him now is on TV. I try not to watch any games that Vegas plays, but hockey is all around me. A lot of players tone it down when they retire and move into a coaching role. Not my father. Sometimes it's hard to avoid catching sight of his handsome face in an interview. Or worse splashed across a tabloid, his arm draped around his perfectly made-up blond wife that's closer to my age than his. Those are the worst. They always throw my mom into a spiral. And that's why I can't be a hockey wife or even a girlfriend. No matter how much Aspen means to me. I've seen what that lifestyle does.

"I've gotta go. Aspen needs help with the car. Love you, Mom."

"Please hurry." She gets in the last word before the call drops out.

My elbows drop to my knees, supporting my bowed head, and I just sit there. That conversation sapped my energy and drained the pleasant warmth from my body.

# Chapter Sixteen

## Aspen

I shift on my feet, hovering by the bathroom door for a moment before backing away. I'm familiar with this conversation, and I know it won't end well for either of us. Jordan will retreat into her head and likely push me away, and the more I think about that, the less happy I am.

My chest swells with emotions that I can't seem to shove back down in the dark hole where they belong. Think of your career. Think of her. Falling for her is a terrible idea. I've always known this, and I've always kept things platonic. The problem is. Now that we've been together, I don't think I can just go back to being friends. I want more. Even if it tears me apart, I'm ready to embrace the coming tornado.

The lump in my throat makes it hard to swallow when I think of what she must be feeling right now. I yank some clothes out of my travel bag, tossing them on and heading for the door.

I wander the floral atrocity that is the main floor of the bed-and-breakfast on a hunt for the spicy old lady that's hosting us. My eyes narrow and a thought itches at my brain as I pass from empty room to empty room.

The scents of vanilla and chocolate lead me to the jackpot. Our host is in a warm yellow room rocking out to music I can't hear. I stretch my arms up to the top of the door frame, crossing one foot over the other as I lean back to wait, not wanting to startle her and cause a cardiac incident. She's got a wooden spoon in her hand and is shaking her booty in a pair of bright pink jogging pants. Add that to the list of things I may never unsee.

Finally, she spins around, jumping when her corn-flower eyes land on me. Thankfully, her heart seems to still be thumping away.

She pulls an Air Pod out of her right ear. "Young man, you shouldn't sneak up on an old lady." Her thin lips are painted bright pink and twisted with humor as she runs her eyes up and down my length. I kinda feel like an animal at the zoo the way she looks at me.

I throw my hands up in front of me. "Give a guy a break, Norma. I was standing here specifically so I didn't scare the shit out of you."

"I guess you're forgiven. Now what can I do for you? You didn't come here just to watch the show." She gives another little wiggle of her hips. "I'm sure you've got better things to do with that young lady of yours."

I roll my eyes. This again. I mean. It might be true this time, but... "I wanted to do something nice for Jordan, but my resources here are limited. Do you have any hot chocolate I could make for her?" Chocolate is only second to books in Jordan's eyes. I pair the request with a smile that goes all the way to my eyes. If this spicy old lady is going to objectify me, I may as well take full advantage of it.

Her eyes light up. "Of course. I can whip some up for you."

Excellent. "Any chance I can help?" Feels like it might mean more if I actually help.

"Of course." She arches a brow at me. "You could reach up there to get the chocolate chips." She points to the highest cupboard above the oven. There's a twinge below my right rib cage when I reach for the white door stenciled with more flowers and pull it open to find... casserole dishes?

"You're sure it's up there?"

I turn to catch her staring at me again. "Oh, my mistake. The chocolate is over here."

She yanks open the door to her left, pulling out a bag of chocolate chips and a tin of cocoa powder.

"Norma, were you checking me out?"

"I don't get too many young men here, especially hockey players. You'll have to forgive me." Not a hint of pink colors her cheeks. The woman has no shame. The guys would love her. She should be our team mascot. We'll have to arrange a visit when the season's over. I can picture Jax, Seb, and Beau competing for her affection. Well maybe Seb not so much now.

She heats some milk on the stove while I try not to spill the chocolate and sugar all over the place as I measure it out.

"Now, have you and your lovely friend finally done the deed?"

A snort has the bag of sugar falling to the counter. "You don't ask strangers things like that."

"I think I just did. My house. My rules." She gestures for me to pour the chips into the pot as she continues to whisk.

"Jordan and I are just friends. We've got different goals. She wants to stay around here and I'm going to go pro. She deserves a guy who will be there for her every day, and I can't promise that."

"I didn't ask if you should. I asked if you did."

The chips slowly melting into the milk have me in a trance as I mull over her words. No idea why, but I kind of want to confess to someone. "Maybe, but if you tell her I told you that, you're cut off. No visits or autographs after I make the NHL." I can't look at her as I say the words.

"I knew it." She crows, dropping the whisk to clap her hands together with glee. She places a hand on my biceps, giving me an intense look. "Now, what are you going to do about it?"

My hand closes over the smooth surface of the whisk as I pick up the task she abandoned. "What do you mean? We're gonna go home and things will go back to normal."

"No, no, no. Unacceptable. You're clearly in love with her. You know you only get one chance at love. Once it's gone, it's gone forever." Her eyes glaze over with a faraway look and my heart twists at the grief I see in those depths. The look's gone in an instant and her hand slams into the back of my head with surprising force. "Get over your shit and get your head out of your ass." I wince, rubbing at the sore spot on the back of my head while trying to stifle a laugh. She's got a decent arm for an old witch.

Love. That's a pretty fucking life changing word dropped before her unexpected string of curses. I definitely love Jordan, but do I love, love her? The sharp throb in my chest at the thought of losing her is my answer. I do. It explains why I've hated every guy she's ever been with. Did I scare a few of them off on purpose? Maybe. Do I regret it for a second? Nope.

The revelation doesn't change anything though. It's only going to make it harder when we have to go back to business as usual.

The oven's piercing beep cuts through my reverie. Norma slides on some oven mitts covered in sunflowers. My lips curve up at the sight of Jordan's favorite flowers as she slides a tray of chocolate chip cookies out of the oven. I'm going to have to hit the gym extra hard to work off all the unapproved food. Too bad fucking your best friend doesn't count on my training plan. Corbin's head would probably explode if I tried to add it. Our fitness trainer's sense of humor is about as good as a hungry grizzly's. He kinda looks like one, too.

"You can take a plate up with your hot chocolate if you get three mugs from the top shelf there." She points to the corner cabinet, and I tilt my head in question. She better not be messing with me again.

"Well, go on."

I open the cupboard, reaching for the matching cups on the bottom shelf. "No, no. The ones on the top shelf. Those are the teacups." A likely story.

I stretch up to the top shelf to grab some chipped black mugs that look like rejects from the thrift store bin, placing them back on the counter with a thunk. I'm going to have to check the back of my shirt when I'm done to make sure her eyes didn't burn a hole through the back.

"You happy?" I ask her.

"Very," she says, using a ladle to spoon a healthy portion in each of the three mugs.

I raise an eyebrow at her. "Not planning on serving any to the other guests?" The guilty look gives her away.

"No. They're probably busy."

"Uh-huh." I snag a cookie off the tray and jam the scalding sugary goodness in my mouth, blowing out to ease the burn.

She puts together a tray with a plateful of cookies and two mugs, shoving it into my hand before shooing me off. "Get back to your girl."

I walk away casually, pausing in the doorway to glance at the devious woman over my shoulder.

"Norma. There aren't any other guests here right now, are there?"

Her wicked smile tells me all I need to know. She's been playing us harder than UM in the final game of the Frozen Four. She shrugs her shoulders, stuffing her headphones back in with a wink and shimmying off with a wiggle of her hips.

I knew it. She's been scamming us. Playing matchmaker the whole time. This woman I've never met before knows me better than I know myself. I shake my head and bound up the stairs, keeping the tray steady the entire time.

# Chapter Seventeen

## Jordan

E ven with the floral clutter, the room feels empty without Aspen. It's like this has become our own little nest in only a day, and I miss him when he's not here. Especially after that conversation with my mom, which, as usual, reinforced my commitment to avoid any sort of long-term relationship. Love might provide an amazing high at first, but it always ends in pain, as I've seen time and again.

I reach for my ultimate comfort blanket, picking up the new book Aspen was perusing the other day. Book boyfriends. They never let you down. Fictional men are the answer. Well, other than the fact that they're merely ink on paper. I'll admit that poses a few constraints.

I've devoured a third of it when the click of the door opening pulls me out of the fictional world and back to reality.

Aspen pushes through with a tray of something that smells like a cold winter night in the kitchen with his mom. "Mmmm…"

Before I can swing my legs over the side of the bed to follow my nose to the deliciousness, he shakes his head at me. "I come bearing chocolate." His cute eyebrow bob has me laughing. The tension that never quite loosened its grip on my shoulders finally eases up at his goofy expression. That face always brings me a smile.

"Gimme, gimme." I don't even know what it is, but I want it. The FMC of the book I was reading is a baker, and it turns out if you read about experimental cupcake flavors for too long, you start craving something sweet. It should really come with a warning. And maybe a cupcake. Now that would be some fun marketing. I bet there's a local bakery I can team up with on that idea.

He places the tray on the bed with a deep bow. "Milady. The finest of hot chocolate prepared by yours truly, along with a side of the world's best chocolate chip cookies."

Her mouth screws up, and she pushes her lips out. "Really? You cooked something for me?" I can't resist the urge to bend down and take that doubting lower lip in between my teeth in a quick nip.

"You doubt me? I'm wounded. I can cook."

"Aspen, I watched you explode a pizza pocket in the microwave. Remember how I almost called CSI to investigate the crime scene?"

I shrug at her. "I hit an extra zero. It could happen to anyone."

"Your nine-year-old sister can cook a pizza pocket."

"Willow is very advanced for her age."

"Uh-huh. Keep telling yourself that."

Who am I kidding? I can't lie to her. Her intense stare has me squirming until I fold like a dog-eared corner under the pressure. She knows me way too well. "Norma did it, but I helped. You can ask her." Although I'm not sure if we can trust anything that sneaky old woman says. I might keep that fact to myself for now. No point letting Jordan know we don't need to share a bed for another night. I'm not strong enough to give up one more night buried so deep inside her that I send her into next week. Fuuuuccck. Even thinking about it has me hard.

I take a huge gulp of hot chocolate to get my mind off that thought. Save it for later.

"Are you ok?" I ask her as she nibbles at a cookie. Her tongue flicking out to clean up a crumb has my dick twitching again. Down boy. Not the time.

Her emerald eyes meet mine. "I'm fine. Just the usual. Mom's man of the week broke up with her."

I know. I've helplessly watched her suffer. If there was anything I could do to make it all better for her, I would, but I know there's nothing. I pull her into my arms, dropping a kiss in her silky hair as I take a deep inhale of her sweet vanilla scent. That's why the cookies made me think of her.

She pulls away to resume her munching. "So, you cooked with Norma. How was that?"

I go along with her change of subject, knowing she needs a distraction. "Devious old woman. She had me reaching for the tallest cupboard only to find out. Surprise. That's not where the chocolate chips were."

Her pale brow quirks with curiosity. "Well, she's getting older. People get forgetful."

"Oh no. She was checking out my ass. I'm just a piece of meat to her. Shocking, really."

Her mirth bubbles out, leaving me toasty warm on the inside.

"Can you blame her?"

"Absolutely not. I'm stunning." I puff out my chest, preening.

And just like that, things are back the way they should be. Aspen and Jordan.

# Chapter Eighteen

## Aspen

M y blood is still buzzing from the sugar high when I drag her outside for a snowball fight. The flakes are tumbling down at a slower rate, but there's still so much of the white stuff I'm not going to risk leaving today. Tomorrow. Maybe. Maybe not. I could stay here forever with her. My head whips back at the force of the cold projectile slamming into it.

"That's it. You're in for it." I struggle through the knee-deep drifts, scooping her up before she can escape. She kicks at me as I throw her over my shoulder with a slap on that fucking incredible ass. Having seen her bared for me I, I know that even my most lurid dreams didn't live up to the reality. I could get addicted to her body.

She's convulsing with giggles, slamming her hands on my back. "Let me go."

"Nope. You need to be taught a lesson."

I fall to the ground, twisting in midair to take the hit on my side, quickly rolling over to prevent her escape with my larger body. Her eyes widen, and she's shaking her head as I scoop up a huge handful of snow, holding it inches from her face. The freckles scattered across the bridge of her cute little nose are practically begging me to kiss them, but nope, that would mean giving up. She's not getting away that easily. "Do you give?"

"Never." She's going for fierce and defiant with narrowed eyes and pursed lips. But all I can see is the sparkle of laughter gleaming in her eyes, so I shove the snow in her face until she's squealing. "Fine. Fine. I give up. Let me go."

Random flashes of light bring out golden glints in her green eyes, and there's snow clinging to the tips of her strawberry eyelashes. I can't resist leaning in, pressing my icy lips to hers.

Her squeals turn to a soft moan as she returns the kiss, her tongue darting out to slide along mine. We clash in a war of tussling tongues and grasping hands, seeking a connection that's impossible under these conditions.

The frozen world around us melts away, and it's just the two of us in this perfect moment in time. Like we're frozen in a snow globe, safe in our bubble of swirling flakes. Lips and hands and... freaking winter coats getting in the way of the good stuff.

"Too...many...clothes." I mumble the words between kisses.

She has zero objections to that sentiment, reaching for her zipper. I still her hand. "Umm, maybe I should get you inside first."

She lets out a frustrated growl as if she's in my head. I can usually be a patient man, but everything feels urgent today. I'm going to savor every second of our time here if this is the only chance I'm gonna get.  I want to imprint every freckle, every inch of skin, every kiss in my memory, so I never forget this lost weekend.

# Chapter Nineteen

## Jordan

Cool air washes over my sweat-sticky body as I pull off my heavy winter clothes, hanging my coat in the front closet. I grab a couple of hangers, sending the rest of them rattling in the almost empty space. There are only two other coats. A bright red puffy one, and a windbreaker with a color block pattern in a palette of garish fluorescents. Why anyone would send that forward in a time machine from the eighties, I don't know. But there's absolutely no other reason I can fathom why that would exist in the twenty-first century.

"Shhhh." I try to hush Aspen as he leads the way down the hall, even though I'm the one giggling so hard the rest of the guests can hear me from upstairs.

My eyes narrow, and I look around the empty place. We haven't seen a single soul aside from Norma since we got here. "It's weird we haven't seen any other guests around, isn't it?"

Aspen's laughter quiets and the right side of his mouth twists down the tiniest bit. I'm no poker player, but we've been best friends for so long I know all his tells. He bumps into me as I stop, spinning around to look him in the eyes. Ouch, all that muscle is going to leave a bruise. "What are you hiding from me?"

He jerks back a little, eyes wide. "What are you talking about?"

I reach up to poke him in that spot at the right corner of his mouth. The little dent that pops up when he's not being entirely honest. "I know when you're lying to me."

"I'm not lying." The words come out way too fast.

Words are not necessary to break him down. He crumbles under my unwavering stare like those delicious chocolate chip cookies he "made."

He flings his hands up in the air. "Ok, but in my defense, I only just found out myself."

He's glancing everywhere but at me. Maybe I have a future as an FBI interrogator. Can only read and interrogate one person. Should probably stick to the bookstore thing.

His face scrunches up and he looks up at the ceiling, blowing out a breath. "There are no other guests here."

"What? So we've been sharing a room, a bed, for..." I almost said no reason, but I mean, those were some pretty compelling reasons he gave me earlier. Multiple reasons, you might say.

"I told you the woman was devious." He hesitates for a moment, searching my face. "Do you want me to ask her for a second room?"

My chest shakes with laughter. "I think we've moved past that. Her plan worked."

His fingers trail down my cheek and his voice goes husky. "It sure did." He dips his head down for a kiss on the nose.

"May as well make use of that one bed while we have the chance. Race ya." I give him a shove and take off for the stairs. I need every advantage I can get. After all, he basically works out for a living. Clearly not a fair race.

He lets me beat him up the stairs and to the door of our room before shoving at me as we jostle to get our keys out. I'm waving mine in his face with a flourish when he sticks his giant shoulder in front of me before I can get it in the lock.

"Cheater."

He's brimming with mock outrage. "Excuse me? I believe you're the one who viciously shoved me out of the way." He opens the door, giving me a view of his tight ass. I don't blame Norma for wanting a look, but I'm the only one who gets to touch it.

"It's only fair I get a head start. Look at those legs." I make the mistake of listening to myself. Those infernal gray sweatpants are taunting me, especially knowing what's underneath them.

His mouth twists in a smirk when he catches me staring. "These legs?" His thumbs hook under the elastic at the waist and he whips them off. It's hot until he trips himself up, trying to get them off his ankles.

He stands there with an eyebrow quirked as I double over in laughter. I'm laughing so hard my stomach hurts, and I can't catch my breath.

"You think that's funny?"

No words can get through my mirth, so I nod. I'm still gasping for air when his hands close around my sides. They slide under my shirt, and I shiver as his roughened fingers scrape against the sensitive skin at my waist.

I'm already melting when he swings me up over his shoulder. The bed is calling to me, so I make a small noise of protest when he turns in the other direction. "Wait. Where are you going?" I raise a hand toward the bed as if I can will us there with my telekinetic powers. That would be a sweet party trick. Telekinetic sex.

"I thought you'd want a shower. You were getting pretty cold out there."

He's not wrong. My fingertips are a little numb now that he mentions it, but the rest of me. The rest of me is on fire.

Every ripple of muscle hits me as I slide down his body. He grips the hem of my shirt, hauling it up and over my head.

"Fuck." There's a deep, dark promise in the single word that slips out through the gravel in his voice.

His hands move up to cup my breasts through my aqua t-shirt bra, dipping his head down between the mounds. He pushes them together around his face, taking a deep inhale. "Too much fabric." The words come out in a desperate rasp as he snaps the back clasp open with way too much skill. He's right. I didn't exactly bring my sexy lingerie for a book trip with my best friend. I kinda wish I had now.

My breasts fall into his powerful hands as if they belong there, released from their supportive prison. I gasp at the sharp bite of pain mixed with pleasure as his thumbs rasp over my nipples, overly sensitized from the cold. I shiver, grabbing at his shoulders to drag him closer even as he pulls away.

"See. You're cold. Need to warm you up." He steps away, sliding open the glass door of the shower.

"But..." The protest dies on my lips as he rips off his shirt, leaning down to turn on the water. His back is a mass of ridges and dips in places I didn't even know you could have muscles. I reach out to stroke a line that runs beneath his right shoulder. "Are you even real?"

There's a laughing, familiar grin on his face when he twists around, but desire deepens his eyes to the color of a shimmering pool deep in the shadowy woods. "I hope so, otherwise I'm going to be very concerned for you."

I take a tentative step toward the shower.

"You planning on showering in those?" His eyes dart away from my tits for the briefest of seconds. "If you need help to take them off, I'm your man." Your man. I like the sound of those words together far too much for my own good.

Pants. Right. Take off my pants for showering. I'm not sure how he managed to dissolve my brain into mush, but apparently, it's a thing. His hands beat me to it when I go for the waistband of my leggings. He slides them down my legs with reverence until my knees are quaking, and

I'm standing in front of him, very aware of my nakedness under the glaring lights of the bathroom. No turning back now. Now we've seen everything. Including that monster cock of his twitching between his thighs, begging for my touch.

He stumbles back onto the smooth surface as my hands shoot out, desperate to touch him. He groans, fumbling with the taps as I make contact.

A shock of icy water stabs at me like tiny needles, and I jump back.

"Shit. Sorry."

He fiddles with the water for another moment, waiting until warms before pulling me under the stream. The heat is heavenly against my chilled skin, but it doesn't compare to the feeling of my body pressed up against his long, lean length. He crushes my breasts against his chest as his mouth descends to capture mine. I run my hands up those cut lines along his back, exploring each hard hill and valley that makes up the map of his back. It's strange I've known this man for fifteen years and yet there's so much more to discover.

I can't resist the silken steel pressing against my abdomen, so I wrap my hand around it. He thrusts his hips to meet my caress with a rumble deep in his throat. I need more. I need to taste him. Every inch of him, but especially his cock.

I slide to my knees, holding on to his thick thighs to keep from slipping on the slick shower floor. His beautiful length jumps toward me as I lean in for a kiss. My tongue darts out to lap up the drop of moisture glistening on the tip, enjoying the salty musk of his essence. His hands tangle in my hair, hanging wet and heavy over my shoulders.

I circle the head before sealing my mouth around it, engulfing him in my wet warmth. His muscles are taut, as if he's trying to restrain himself from thrusting down my throat. I dig my fingers into his hips and pull him close, letting him slide deeper. He takes it as permission to thrust in small, quick movements as my tongue continues to dance along his cock.

My pussy is pulsing with need, so I reach down between my thighs to find the sensitive nub there. I circle my clit in time with his thrusts. Pressure builds in my core.

I'm nothing but need right now. Nothing else matters except this. Us. This feeling. The heat spreads through my entire body until I could spontaneously combust at any moment.

His thrusts are increasing with urgency, but his hands slide to my cheeks in a gentle hold, as if I'm precious to him.

He thickens inside my mouth as I'm riding the edge of my high. My eyes flick up to meet his as he pulls back a bit with a groan until only the full head of him rests inside me.

"I can't wait any longer. I'm gonna come, Jordan."

"Go ahead." My voice is rough and needy.

I take him back inside, desperate for the musky taste of him as I chase my release. My fingers increase their rhythm in time with the speed of his thrusts until my world implodes. I grip his hips tighter as convulsions of pleasure rock my body. He lets out a feral groan as his hot seed hits the back of my throat. I swallow it down as my pussy clenches around nothing. It would be fantastic to be rippling around him, but I'm glad I got to do that. To taste him. Even if it's only this once.

"Jordan." He moans, dragging me up off my knees. My legs threaten to give out underneath me, but he holds me safe and secure. "That was fucking incredible."

# CHAPTER TWENTY

## ASPEN

Holy shit. My cock has never been so ecstatic, and so desperate at the same time. Now that he's had a taste of Jordan's sweet pussy, her devilish mouth. He's never going to crave anyone else. He's addicted, and so am I.

I hold her steady as she quakes with aftershocks, wrapping my arms tight around her. Wanting to keep her beside me forever. It's not just the sex. Although that is fucking incredible. She's my best friend. She's always been there for me, and I hope I've returned the favor. I know she doesn't want my lifestyle, though. The travel, the uncertainty. She's had enough of that over her lifetime. But I want to make this work. I want her beside me forever.

"Well, I'm definitely warm now." Her lips quirk up in a teasing grin.

"I fucking hope so." I growl.

"Maybe not so clean, though."

"Definitely dirty. You're a dirty, dirty girl. I can fix that."

I'm desperate to get my hands back on her smooth skin. To trace and map every single freckle. To claim them as if that's my right. The snack-sized bottle of hotel shampoo looks extra tiny in my giant paws as I squeeze some out. The smell of cranberries surrounds us, intensified by the steamy heat of the water pouring down. Seems like a good excuse to lay hands on her again.

I slide along her smooth skin in long strokes, relishing every second I get to touch her. My time feels very limited. I know she's stuck on the bullshit idea of this only being a weekend away thing. What happens at the B&B stays at the B&B and all that.

She moans, pushing her chest into me as I spend extra time on her perfect breasts. After I've got them thoroughly cleaned, I duck down to lick each rosy nipple. The pale pink nubs are taut again, begging, so I oblige, sucking the tip into my mouth.

"We're never going to get out of here if you keep doing that."

I look up, not releasing her glorious tit. "Maybe that's what I want." I mumble around her soft flesh.

"Not sure you'll still be saying that when the water turns to ice."

I weigh my options. I think I could handle a little deep freeze to spend another moment with my hands on her gorgeous body.

She bobs her eyebrows at me. "Plus, I haven't gotten a chance to clean you yet." Her devilish hands dart down to close over my dick and I groan.

"Are you hard again already? Are you secretly an alien? Shifter? Oooh, vampire? Immortal endurance." The ache intensifies as she punctuates each question with a squeeze.

"You read too many books. I'm an athlete, babe. I've got endurance you could only dream about. Also, pretty sure you could make me hard any time, day, or night." Her pupils dilate until they're a black abyss I could get lost in. Too much? If I tell her how I really feel, she'll probably bolt out of here and walk home. Snowstorm or no snowstorm. I'll find my favorite person encased in a block of ice on my drive home.

"Maybe we should get out of here." My dick is super pissed at me when she loosens her hold.

"You're right. The water is going to get cold. Not to mention Norma will probably be up with dinner soon." Thinking of the nosy yet helpful old lady is enough to calm him down a bit.

I shut off the water and we fight over the same towel. "Always a competition with you." She giggles as she pulls it away. I let her. I'd give her anything. Anything that's mine is hers.

The soft towel feels almost rough against my skin compared to her hands. She picks up a shirt to slide over her head and I hate to see her cover herself up, but it's probably necessary. "Wait." She gives me a curious look as I lay a hand over hers to prevent her from finishing the job. "You should wear this." I toss her my jersey. She used it to break me down in the first place. Now she needs to reap the consequences of her actions.

She grabs it from me with a smirk. "What. You expect me to wear this the rest of our time here?"

"Yup." I pop the p. "You are mine after all." My voice drops again on that word that sounds so right. She is mine. She's always been mine. It was meant to be.

"Fine." She takes it. "I'll be yours." She leaves the last words unspoken, but I can hear the weight of them in her voice. 'For now,' is what she means, when I mean forever.

I've never seen my jersey look so good. My name on her back has every possessive instinct I never knew I had begging to drag her home by her hair. I need to chill the fuck out.

"Maybe I'll go downstairs to grab our dinner. Save Norma the trip."

"Right. Good idea." Her eyes are darting around as if she's already looking for her escape route.

# Chapter Twenty-One

## Jordan

I should be drifting away on a fluffy cloud of joy after that super-hot shower sex. Instead, I'm twitchy and restless. My skin is itchy, and I can't stop pacing around the small room while Aspen is gone.

There was something in his eyes that made me edgy and ready to step into my boots and bolt, or wade, I guess. Given the ridiculous volume of snow out there, my speed would make a snail proud. We agreed on a onetime thing. Or I guess a few times, several times? But only here, in our little haven. We're supposed to go home and go back to being best friends. No benefits. But his touch, his words, and that dark possessiveness in his eyes when he asked me to wear his jersey all scream for keeps. He wants more. Don't get me wrong, I want more too, but we can't have it. It won't work. No matter how hard I try, I can't make the pieces fit together in my head. Me with the bookstore, stability, a home. Him with his dream career as a professional hockey player.

I force myself to sit on the bed, folding my knees up under my chin while my brain searches for a solution. My fingers close over the smooth screen of my phone, and I mindlessly scroll, tapping the Instagram icon. A smile blooms on my face as I land on his account. Pictures of him playing hockey, goofing off with the guys. His arms slung around Sebastian and Jackson. And girls. The smile fades when I see the girls. That's what the hockey life is all about. Girls, women, in constant pursuit, seeking to bask in the light of his fame even if it's only for a moment, for a night.

I know because my dad was like that when he was with Mom. He cheated on her with any puck bunny that happened across his path while on the road. I was too young to understand back then, but as I got older, I saw the pictures, the articles. His careless lack of fidelity shattered her. And she's never gotten over it. She hops from man to man, moving us around, trying to make herself the perfect woman for her current boyfriend, never thinking about herself and what she wants. Or me. I don't want that for myself, and I really couldn't bear it if that destroyed my friendship with Aspen. He's been a constant in my unstable life. Him and the bookstore, which we've held onto through all of Mom's whims and moves.

This is why book boyfriends are better. No complications. I'd never admit it on my book blog, but I've always preferred the friends to lovers trope rather than the enemies to lovers that's so popular right now. And it's finally dawning on me why. I'm in love with my best friend... FML.

God, what am I going to do? Why did I think this was a good idea? I thought we could do this thing. Make it fun and uncomplicated. I'm the one who coerced him into it. Not that he didn't want it, but he was afraid too. He was afraid of feeling more, and that's what I've been afraid of, only for different reasons. I love him, but we can't be together.

What have you done, Jordan?

# Chapter Twenty-Two

## Aspen

"I really appreciate you cooking all these meals for us. You didn't have to do that. We could have scrounged something up."

Norma flutters her hand in a dismissive wave. "Of course I do. You think I'd let guests in my house starve? Besides, you need lots of protein to keep those muscles strong." She eyes me like she'd enjoy taking a bite of my biceps. Good choice, Aspen. I knew this would cool me down after the amazing shower experience I just shared with Jordan. No chance of my friend below perking up when our host is eying me. She's a lovely lady, don't get me wrong. Not exactly my type, though.

"I know. But we could help, or whatever." I finish the thought on a lame note. Could I really help her in the kitchen? Maybe Jordan could. She's learned to look after herself. Me. Not so much. Mom has always spoiled me with her home-cooked meals or food from the family restaurant. I never really had to learn to cook since I was constantly at hockey practice or games or working out. Not exactly the picture of a helpful child.

"You think I'd let you roam free in my kitchen? You didn't even know where to find the chocolate chips?"

She's right not to let me in her domain, but that's hardly fair. "Wait a minute." I hold my hand up. "You're the one who sent me to the wrong cupboard."

Her eyes are twinkling. "Hmmm. Maybe. I'm getting old. Can't trust this brain of mine anymore."

"Uh-huh."

"Everything is ready. I appreciate you coming to carry it all up. Your lady will appreciate it, too."

"Yeah." I'm kinda stuck, hesitating before grabbing the tray she prepped.

"Is something wrong? Aren't you in a hurry to get back to her? Don't let little old me stop you." She narrows her eyes, assessing me with a laser vision that I'm sure can see to the depths of my soul. That look is exactly why I don't believe her earlier comment about her old brain. She's still sharp as a freshly forged blade.

"No, it's fine." I hitch my hip up on the counter, planting myself more firmly instead of leaving like I should.

"Did you mess this up already? I can't do everything for you." Her tone is scolding.

"There was nothing to mess up." I protest.

"Sure. You get back up there and tell her you love her. Every woman deserves to hear that at least ten times a day from her man."

"I don't love her." I protest, but the lie sounds weak even to my own ears. Even if I do, it doesn't matter, right? I'm not good for her.

I've almost convinced myself by the time I'm at the door to our room.

The forced smile feels weird. Here's hoping it resembles my usual grin and not some fake photoshopped excuse for happiness. My eyes seek Jordan as soon as I walk through the door, as if I'm drawn to her like a magnet. I am. She looks so fucking hot in my jersey. Her long creamy legs are folded up to her chin. They're peeking out beneath the rich purple fabric, and I almost can't tear my gaze away to look her in the eyes.

When I do, I realize she's already pulled back. That caged wild animal look is in her gorgeous green eyes. Like she wants to escape this room, this situation, me. Fuck. I shouldn't have left her alone with her thoughts. Nothing good ever comes from that.

"Jordan. Got us dinner. I offered to help Norma, and she laughed in my face."

"Yeah." She agrees. I was hoping for some sort of vehement agreement with Norma over my sad lack of cooking skills or a smile at my fake pout. Anything. But no. She's already shutting me out. Trying to push me away.

"Okay then. Let's eat this dinner." The delicious smell of the homemade meatloaf would normally have me slavering like a stray dog, but Jordan's silence has stolen my appetite.

Fuck. How am I going to fix this?

# Chapter Twenty-Three

## Aspen

There were a few feet of distance between us physically and a few light years emotionally at the start of the night. Jordan blew off my attempt at a kiss with a wide yawn as she slid into bed. The only thing giving me the slightest bit of hope is that she's still draped in my jersey.

This morning, I woke up with her twined around me as if we gravitated toward each other in our sleep. Her unconscious mind is the only part of her that will let her get close to me.

I made the mistake of pulling her in to bury my face in her tangled curls with a kiss. There's an ache in my chest thinking this could be my only chance at this. Unfortunately, it woke her up, and she rolled away, putting some distance back between us. My arms felt extra empty after that.

My phone lets out an irritating buzz and she fumbles for it, glancing at the screen before looking at me, her face drooping with resignation. "It's your coach. We definitely need to get home today."

She's right. The snow stopped overnight, and I'm sure they've cleared the major roads by now. We can make it home, but I don't want to. First time in my life I'm not excited to get back to hockey after a few days off. I grab my phone from her.

"Ellory!" I wince at the bark coming through the line. "I better see your ass at practice this afternoon."

I nod. Yeah, I need to get back. Hockey will take my mind off Jordan anyway. His words remind me why this can't work. We want different things, and she deserves all her dreams to come true. Stability, love. Fury builds inside at the thought of her in love with another guy. The kind of rage usually reserved for a dirty hit on my goalie. But when you love someone, you want them to be happy, right? Turns out feelings are way more complicated than that.

"Looks like we're going to be sweating to clear the way out of here. I'll get started."

I clear my throat and get up. She averts her eyes from my naked body as I throw clothes on. "I'm just gonna have a shower."

A groan slips out at her words, and my already hard dick reminds me of our shower yesterday. Digging us out of this shitstorm of snow will cool him down.

"Now don't be strangers. I want a visit and an autograph once you get drafted. Maybe a picture to hang on the wall."

"Of course, Norma. Thanks so much for looking after us."

"My pleasure. It's not every day I get to host a future NHLer. Plus, you shoveled the drive for me. I almost think I should give you a discount, but nah. It was good for you. Keep those muscles in tiptop shape."

I laugh, leaning in for a side hug. She turns her head to plant a big smack on my cheek.

"See you soon."

Jordan gets folded into her flowery embrace next. "You look after this guy. Make sure his head doesn't get too big once he's famous."

"Sure, Norma." Her reply doesn't contain much conviction.

"Let's go, Jordan." It takes the air out of me like a hard hit to the boards when her arm crosses over her body to rub a shoulder, avoiding the hand I hold out.

I don't think I've ever had an awkward silence with Jordan. Not once. Ever since that time she defended me in the kindergarten yard, we've been tight. I introduced her to hockey. She's a rabid hockey fan now. Like, she was the overly involved parent yelling at the refs at my games as a kid, since my parents didn't have the time to be there. Best part is no one could get mad at the adorable redhead with the pigtails. She got away with so much shit. The thought of feisty little Jordan curves my lips up in a small smile.

She introduced me to books and though our tastes have veered apart, I'll always be thankful for the time spent at her bookstore. After my parents bought the attached restaurant, I spent any time I had off the rink at Top Shelf. And she always picks a book out for me before away games. Most of the guys play video games or card games on the bus. Me. I'm always reading. Although I have converted a couple of them.

"That was fun?" Man, I'm really losing my touch if that's my attempt at conversation.

"Yeah," she says, pointedly putting her book down and her headphones in, effectively shutting down any further conversation.

I can't stand this distance between us.

Massive snowbanks piled high by the side of the roads are the only sign of the record-breaking snowstorm that just hit us. It's a reasonable drive, so my shoulders are tense for a very different reason than the drive to the Knotty Pine. Every mile seems to increase the distance Jordan is putting between us.

My brain's racing to find ways to prolong the trip. I'm afraid she's going to slip through my fingers once we're separated. "Wanna grab something to eat before I drop you off?"

She ignores me, so I pluck the purple earbud out of her ear. "Hey, wanna grab some food? Tacos?" I add, hoping her favorite food will tempt her.

Her eyes dart to mine before shifting away. "I really should get home. Mom needs my help. And you've got practice."

She's got me there. Yeah, I don't want to think about how Coach will choose to punish me if I don't show up, but I would have dipped out on it for a last chance to be with her.

Shit. That is not the attitude I'm going to need to finish this year strong. Sure, Pittsburgh drafted me, but I decided to complete my degree. Hockey doesn't last forever, right? I turned down the contract they offered me after sophomore year. It felt like the right decision, but it's left me in a precarious spot. They might still pick me up as a free agent after graduation, but I'm really hoping for Chicago. That's been my dream since I was teetering around in the Mini Mites. I've always vowed not to let a girl get between me and that dream. Not like Dad did.

I slide out of my car after pulling into her driveway, trying to string together the words to convince her to stay with me. She tries to brush me off when I reach for her bag, but I ignore her attempt to grab it.

"I can carry your bag."

"I know."

The words don't come until we're standing on her porch. She tries to steal her bag away and I don't let her.

"Listen. I don't want to lose you."

"You're not going to lose me." She's still not meeting my eyes. "I need to go. Mom, you know."

Oh, I know all about her mom. I know she's had her own struggles, but it guts me how she's put everything on her daughter. It's too much. Too much for a kid to handle.

I tug on her bag, trying to pull her back to me. I don't know if I wanna steal one last kiss or declare my love for her, no matter how ill advised that would be for both of us, but she pulls back.

"Please, Jordan..."

# Chapter Twenty-Four

## Jordan

An insistent ring interrupts whatever he was about to say. "You should get that."

His shoulders are hunched with tension, and he swallows hard before glancing down and up, then back down again. I want to reach out and brush those curls of sandy hair that have fallen into his eyes. He always waits too long to get a haircut.

"Hello?"

I can't hear the words, but the voice shouting through his cell is unmistakable. His coach. Of course. That steels my resolve. Hockey comes first. Hockey always comes first, which is how it should be. It's his passion. His world. He's neglecting it for me, and that's not right. He was meant to play. He's going to be famous. And he deserves it. Everything he's worked for.

"Yeah, I'm on my way. Just dropping Jordan off."

"Uh-huh."

"Bye."

He loosens his hold on my bag, and I take advantage of the slack, tugging it away. "Thanks for the ride." Completely inadequate sentiment, but I don't know how to express my feelings.

"Hey. I'll call you later." The words he calls at my retreating form are a gentle caress that almost has me turning around.

"Sure." The click of my key in the lock has a feeling of finality to it. I don't look back until I make it inside. Leaning against the front door, peeking through the small window.

He's already pulling out of the drive. A preview of where we'll be at the end of the school year. There's an ache in my heart that I'm not sure I'll ever recover from, but the longer I stay with him, the worse it will be when he leaves me for good. I may as well start cutting ties now.

"Honey! You're home. Finally."

An unfamiliar wave of lavender engulfs me with her dramatic hug. She's always changing her perfume, so she never has that distinctive scent that takes me back to my childhood. I miss that rosy smell with a hint of lemon that used to follow her in a cloud of comfort. She stopped wearing that scent after my father left us. I check out the long, flowered skirt swirling around her ankles.

"Hi, Mom."

"Listen. Can you work at the store tomorrow after school? Annika called in sick, and I already have plans."

I hold in the weary sigh, nodding into her chest. "Sure, Mom." Nice to see you too.

At least it'll give me some time to tinker with my new plan. Operation bring the store into the 21st century.

# Chapter Twenty-Five

## Aspen

Pain radiates from my shoulder all the way to my fingertips and the thundering roar tosses my brain around my skull.

"What's wrong with you, Woodsy? You're distracted AF. Thinking about a girl?" Dev gives me another shove, grinding me into the boards before letting me up.

"Ellory! Office after practice."

If any words are going to put the fear of God in a man, it's those particular words coming out of those lips. Coach doesn't put up with any of our shit and he definitely doesn't have the patience for us if we're distracted.

Get your head together. I tell myself, taking a deep inhale of the cool scent of the arena. I shake arms out and focus on the puck. We're playing a scrimmage short, and I haven't been doing my side any favors.

I shove Jordan out of my brain, push off across the ice, heading straight for Jax. He thinks they've got the win on this, so he's fooling around with some intricate footwork. Looks like a fancy figure skater.

He's not expecting me on his left side, so it's easy to swipe the puck from between his skates and I take off like the lightning our team is named for.

I fake to the left and then shoot high and right. It sneaks in over Mitchy's glove, and he curses me out.

A smile spreads across my face. I can still play, even with a hole the size of Texas in my chest. My shoulders fall as the ache throbs. Ever since I was old enough to lace up my own skates, hockey has been my world. But Jordan was always a part of that world. I was too stupid to realize it until recently. And now, for the first time in my life, hockey is not quite enough.

My eyes wander from the whiteboard listing our roster to the picture of Coach's wife and two daughters on the desk. Anywhere but at the man himself. "Aspen. You pulled yourself together at the end, but you know you can't afford any distractions. If this girl is a distraction, fix it. I gave you that time off on the condition you came back sharp and ready to play."

"I know, sir. It won't be a problem." And it won't. Jordan is pulling away. It's best for both of us.

"It better not be. You turned down that contract to finish school. Risky move, but I respect it. Not to mention I'd hate to lose you so soon. You're one of the best that's been through here. Don't squander your chance."

His praise warms the aching hollow. Not his usual style. Dropping compliments like he's got a quota on them.

"I won't."

The guys are gonna give me so much shit when I get home after getting called into Coach's office, but I duck out quickly to put it off as long as possible. Maybe they'll have found something else to satisfy their voracious appetites for gossip.

I'm absently scrolling when I find a meme of a cat eating a slice of pizza with the caption "Uh-Oh." I've typed in 'Coach's office' and hit send before my brain catches up with my fingers. Is she even going to answer? This is our thing. I keep her posted on my day. Small things, big things, silly memes, and serious questions. She humors me and always replies. Who will I text bomb if she isn't around? Who's going to pick books for me to read on road trips?

# CHAPTER TWENTY-SIX

## JORDAN

"Earth to Jordan." Jazz's smooth voice cuts through the reverie I sunk into after I got another text from Aspen. He's been keeping me up to date on his hockey stuff and sending me random memes and tidbits from his day. It's like our usual conversation except I haven't been answering him. I've started wincing every time my phone buzzes.

"What, sorry?"

"You were telling me about your progress on taking Top Shelf online. I think it's a fab plan. World domination is imminent."

I smile at my friend. She works at the best campus coffee shop, but she's planning on opening her own place after graduating with her commerce degree. She's floated the idea of going into business together. Opening a joint coffee shop/bookstore. I love her passion, and I know she's going to succeed, but I can't leave Mom in the lurch. If I'm being honest with myself, it's more about keeping the bookstore running. The one certainty from my childhood.

"Okay. So, I met Melanie Arbour at the conference, and she's super excited about working with a local indie bookstore. Her next release is in six months, and she was very receptive to working with us to provide personalized signed copies. It would be an exclusive deal."

"That's freaking amazing. I knew you'd make some incredible contacts there, but that is beyond anything. I wish I could have come."

If only. If only I had brought Jazz instead. We would have had a fantastic time, and maybe Aspen and I could have avoided making a mess of our friendship. "You don't even know how much I wish it was you." I drop a hand on top of hers, needing some sort of contact without my usual human comfort blanket to rely on.

"What's wrong, hon?" She dips her head, trying to meet my gaze while I blink rapidly to fight back the tears.

"It's nothing." I ignore the burning behind my eyes and bite my bottom lip to keep it from wobbling under her penetrating stare.

"It's obviously not nothing. You've got this great thing going on with the store, so what is it? Your Mom? Do you have to move again?"

It's a good guess. I only met Jazz in freshman year, but talking to her has the comfortable familiarity of someone you've known your entire life. She's the only one aside from Aspen that knows everything that's gone on with my mom and the constant moving.

"No. She's fine. For now."

Her dark eyes narrow, and her lips purse in an I'll-help-you-bury-the-body kind of way. "Is it Aspen? Did he mess with you? I'll fight him for you. Break off that hockey stick of his and stab him with it."

A shaky laugh slips past the pain in my heart. "No, it wasn't him. It was me."

"Honey. I'm sure it's not your fault. What did he do?"

I throw my hands over my face, squeezing my eyes tight, so I don't have to look at my friend. "I kinda tricked him into sleeping with me."

Her snort has me peeking through my fingers. "Tricked him? Um. I don't think so. He looks at you the way I look at Mint Chocolate ice cream. Desperate to eat it, but afraid of the consequences. That boy has wanted to sleep with you...," she pauses, squinting and staring at the ceiling, "since he realized that was a thing he wanted to do."

"What? No. We're friends. We've always been friends. It's not like that."

"Okay. I'm gonna need more of the story before I make my judgement on whether to kill him slowly or make it a quick death."

"You don't need to kill him at all. We got stuck at this B&B because of the snowstorm. He looked so freaking hot. I couldn't resist, but he was being careful, cautious. So, I put on his jersey..." I trail off until she glares me down from under her perfectly arched black brow, "and nothing else." I whisper the last words, looking over her shoulder.

"Nice! What's the problem? Did he ditch you afterward? Is he ghosting you? Was it terrible? Where is he?" She grabs her massive purse with the colorful daisies on it from under the table, wielding it like a weapon as she rises from her chair.

"No. None of that. Sit." I tug her sleeve. "It was amazing." The ghost of the memory sends shivers down my spine. "He was amazing, but then I remembered why it can't happen. You know the whole future professional hockey player situation? He's going to move to some place far away, maybe even Canada, and travel all the time. That's not what I want."

The murderous sheen in her eyes softens to a compassionate glow. "Haven't you talked to him about this?"

"No. I can't. These feelings aren't going away. I'll give in, and then what? What happens next year? He'll be gone and I'll be a brokenhearted mess. Better to end it now."

"Hon, you know I love you, but you need to deal with this. You're into him. He's your best friend. And if you're in love with him, then you deserve to explore that." Her soft hand is warm and reassuring when she covers mine.

"And then?"

"You work it out. Don't turn your back on love to avoid potential heartbreak. The way I look at it, you get a finite number of chances at love. If you squander them?" Her fingers blow up like an explosion. "Too bad. They're gone. And even if you don't pursue that kind of relationship, can you picture your life without him?"

The picture that pops into my head is bleak. What if he's not there? What if he stops sending me ridiculous memes, and telling me the raunchy joke Jackson told him in the locker room? Our lives are tangled together so tightly I don't even know how to exist without him.

"At least talk to him. You owe that to him and yourself. I love you, and that's why I need to be straight with you. There aren't enough good guys out there." Jazz tenses up for a moment. "He's one of them. Don't lose him."

She's right. He's one of the best people I know. Kind, compassionate, hardworking, and the most loyal friend ever. And I'm in love with him. I've been searching for stability in a place, but when it comes right down to it, he's it. My anchor. My safe house. I can't lose him.

"What if... What if it's too late? What if he doesn't want to see me?"

"I guess you'll have to do something big. To let him know you mean it."

Right. Something big.

# Chapter Twenty-Seven

## Aspen

"Woodsy, dude, what is wrong with you? You've been such a downer since you got back last weekend. Ruining my high from the win." Jackson's eyes are wandering to a couple of blond chicks eye fucking him from the bar even as he gives me crap. I'm kind of regretting coming out with the team to Wright's tonight. I should have stayed home.

The guys never made fun of my name. Not like that jerk in elementary school, but Jax called me Woodsy the first time we met in freshman year, and it stuck. Jordan is the only one around here who uses my actual name. I should be ecstatic about our win too, but she hasn't answered any of my texts all week, and it's really bringing me down. And she wasn't at the game, cheering me on. I may have taken some of my frustration out on UM tonight, playing a little rougher than usual. I rub at my aching right shoulder.

"Can't talk about it."

That pulls his attention from the girls he's set his sights on. "You can't talk about it? That's bullshit. Team is family. You can tell me anything. Don't be like that asshole." He glances over at Seb, but his pinched eyebrows tell me it's worry, not anger, that has him commenting. I'd probably be a brooding asshole if I was out all season, too. I feel for the guy, but he is not handling his injury well.

Sighing, I drag a hand down my face. "I slept with Jordan. When we got stranded by the storm."

"Finally!! About damn time you tapped that. She's hot."

My right hook rocks him back on his heels. "Don't talk about her like that, asshole."

"Ow!" He rubs his shoulder, lips pursed. "Uncalled for. I was stating a fact. Wait, so is this? Are you in luuurv with her?" Immature doofus sings out the words like a kindergartner.

My glare seems to speak volumes.

"You are? That's fantastic. I fucking love Jordan." He jerks away and throws up his hands in surrender at my narrowed eyes. "Not like that. Don't hit me again. I would never go there. I have zero desire to end my hockey career before it's started. No. I mean, she's a delight. For you. Seriously, chill. Why are you here with us jerks when you could be enjoying that sweet ass?"

I stare at the chandelier made entirely of empty beer bottles hanging over us, counting to ten so I don't hit my friend again. I don't really want to share with the class, but Jackson is my closest friend after Jordan. Him and Seb, of course, but Seb's dealing with his own shit at the moment. Or not dealing with it. "She ditched me. When things got too intense, she got scared and ran."

"And?" Jackson looks at me as if I'm a moron.

"What do you mean, and? She's not returning my texts or calls. I can't force her to love me back."

"Hard to force the willing, man. You two were the world's cutest platonic married couple. Now that you've fucked her." My hands curl into fists at his crass words, and he shows me his palms. "Don't hit me again. Slept with her? Made love to her? Is that better? Anyway. Now that you've done the deed, you can move on and be the happy couple you were destined to be. The snowstorm was like fate or some shit like that."

"She won't return my texts. How exactly do I to do that?"

He gives me that you're-an-idiot look again. "What, am I supposed to fix all your problems for you? I'm not your mom, dude. I'm sure you can find a way. Go get her." He waves me off. "I've got someone else to catch, maybe two someones if I'm extra lucky." All I see is the back of his shaggy blond head as he struts off toward the girls.

Fuck if he's right, though. What am I even doing here? I need to get my girl.

My fingers drum out an incessant beat on the Uber ride over to her place. I'm halfway out the door before the car comes to a complete halt.

"Hey." The driver calls at my running back. Shit. He's gonna give me a bad rating. Whatever. Totally worth it.

I run up to knock on the chipped paint of the white front door. I should paint that for them. That would be nice, right?

I pause before my fist lands, checking the Cassio on my wrist. Jordan always makes fun of me for wearing an old school watch. Is eleven too late to be pounding on the door? Probably. Her Mom could be asleep and then what kind of asshole would I be? Not the best impression I could make.

I dial her number. It rings and rings straight to voice-mail. Maybe a text?

**Jordan. Can we please talk? I'm here at your front door. Begging if I have to.**

I wait, and wait, and wait some more. Half an hour has passed when I drag myself off her front porch. Don't I look like an idiot standing here, shivering in my game suit?

# Chapter Twenty-Eight

## Jordan

I 've done so many ridiculous things to avoid Aspen this week. Ducking behind a tree on the quad, hopping on a bus I wasn't supposed to be on, and riding it to the next stop. That one made me late for class. But this had to be perfect. I messed up bad. So, I have to pay my penance.

He deserves every iota of my attention and probably a bunch of groveling too. Guilt left me with a severe case of indigestion after his calls and texts last weekend. He was right there, on my porch, but it wasn't the time yet.

I told Mom no for probably the first time ever when she tried to con me into canceling my plans to work at Top Shelf. I've been busting my butt, getting our ecommerce up and running. She can handle it for a couple of days. The revelation that the store isn't my entire life has left my shoulders lighter than they've been in years. I deserve to make my own future. It might be at Top Shelf, or maybe

I'll open my own bookstore wherever Aspen ends up. As long as we're together, things will work out.

Jazz got the weekend off to join me on my quest. They're playing Michigan State, so it's about an hour's drive. I could have done this at a home game, but it feels more significant that I'm traveling for it. It's my way of letting him know I'll be there for him. Wherever he ends up. If he'll forgive me, that is. Icy fingers of dread creep up my back, threatening to cut off my air supply if this fails. If I'm too late.

My entire body buzzes with nerves as we thread through the crowd into the enemy's arena. The rivalry between Lakeview and State is fierce, so I might stand out a little decked in purple and gold head to toe.

Our seats are behind the net Lakeview is defending for the first period.

My Lightning gear stands out against the sea of royal blue, and I shiver as I finger the hem of the jersey, re-membering the last time I wore it. I've got my red curls tamed into a ponytail and buried under a black ball cap pulled low to shadow my face. I made Jazz do the same. It's not time yet, and I don't want to distract him from his game.

They hit the ice with less fanfare than at home, but I can't peel my eyes off him. Number fourteen. That's my man. He moves on the ice like he was born with blades on his feet. Graceful, powerful, fast, and sexy as fuck.

Normally I'd be on my feet shouting when the ref makes a bad call and Beau gets sent to the penalty box.

Not today. Today I'm venting all my anxiety on my poor purple painted nails, chipping away at the polish.

I shake my head at the crinkly bag of popcorn Jazz shoves at me. The toasted butter smell is tempting, but no way the butterflies in my stomach will play nice with arena food.

I'm an anxious bundle of frayed nerves by the end of the first period. The score is tied 1-1. Jackson nabbed the goal for us with an assist from Aspen. They're such a smooth team, gliding across the ice, passing the puck with the intuition of teammates that know each other well. It's beautiful to watch.

They're struggling a bit without Sebastian to support them. Aspen is picking up some of the slack from his center position, but Rory, the right winger that's been pulled onto their line, can't keep up with them. The redheaded senior doesn't have the intuitive connection they usually share. He's decent, but he won't be going pro.

My screwed shut eyes fly open when the boards rattle in front of us. It's Aspen. He's been hit hard. I stand up, reaching toward him, as if I can do anything to help. One of those knee-jerk reactions, like trying to press the brake from the passenger seat. He regains his balance, but my movement catches his eye. His mouth falls open when he meets my worried stare. Then it curls into a huge smile behind his cage. He slams his stick into the glass, pointing at me.

A waterfall of snow showers the glass as he pushes off like a rocket. It takes me a minute to spot the puck. Lakeview's D men are fighting hard to keep it away from their goal. I eye the red numbers ticking down the last couple of minutes.

Connell and Whitaker are currently on the ice defending. "Come on!" I shout, finally letting loose. He knows I'm here now, so I might as well.

Connell finally chips it loose from State's left winger and shoots it up the ice. Aspen is ready for it. He snatches the puck and takes off, passing it to Jax and muscling around number ten that was pressuring him.

He gains a little distance from his tail, and everyone is closing in on Jackson. I'm spitting chips of nail polish out as he pulls his stick back like he's ready to send the puck flying. He makes a lightning-fast change up and shoots it to Aspen, who slams it into the back of the net under the goalie's catcher.

The lamp lights up, and the crowd is screaming. Aspen spins on his skates, looking directly at me with a salute, before rejoining his team. With less than a minute to go, our boys glide around on the ice playing a game of keep away until the clock runs down.

It's close enough to home that we've brought along our fair share of fans. The boos still outweigh the cheers here, but I'm making my throat hoarse trying to out-scream our rivals. I walk right up to the glass. My curls spring free as I rip off my hat and yank out the ponytail holder holding it back. My hands are trembling as I hold up the hand-painted sign.

**YOU MUST ALLOW ME TO**
**TELL YOU HOW ARDENTLY**
**I ADMIRE AND LOVE YOU**

Jazz teased me about the Austen quote. It is a little long for a poster at a hockey game, but Aspen will get it. I made him read P & P one (or five) too many times in our high school years. Mr. Darcy will always be my first love. It seemed appropriate.

Plus, he's not the one that's been fighting his feelings so hard. I recognized that look in his eyes. He would have gone all in if I hadn't fled like I was running from an axe murderer at summer camp.

He breaks free of the dog pile of his teammates, skating over to press his gloved hands to the board in front of me.

"I love you too, Jordan." Everyone near us turns around to stare at me, but I've only got eyes for him.

His words fill up every empty crack in my soul. Every lonely night, every sad day, every abrupt move washes away under the warmth of his gaze. He feels like home.

# CHAPTER TWENTY-NINE

## ASPEN

I can't get off the ice fast enough. As I duck out of the locker room, my hair drips all over my plain black suit. Some guys go for fancier game day attire. Beau is a huge dandy in his custom suit and shiny brown shoes, but I couldn't care less about fashion.

Jackson's still in his towel when he grabs my arm. "Where do you think you're going?"

"To get my girl." I shake him off like a pesky bug.

"Coach is gonna kick your ass when you don't show up for the team bus." I like that he says when not if. He knows how important this is to me. How important she is.

"I don't give a fuck. Let him."

"Your ass." But he grins at me with the shiny white smile that'll have a dozen women dropping their panties for him after the game.

I rush out the door and down the aisle, searching for her. A couple other girls are trying to land a player on the way out but no sign of her bright red hair. Where are you? Phone. I start patting my pockets. Don't be the moron Jackson claimed you were. As I'm sliding my cell out of my pocket, something catches my eye.

A whirlwind of crimson and purple is hurtling toward me. I shake my head at the security guard that's about to do something he'll regret. He's a big dude, but I've been hit by bigger dudes. I can take it and give it right back to him if he dares to lay a hand on my Jordan.

She's leaping through the air with zero doubt that I'll catch her. My hands fly up under her legging clad thighs as she flings her legs around my waist.

We come together in a flurry of kisses that end with us both breathless.

"I'm so sorry." She gets the words out through kiss-reddened lips.

"For what?" I don't even remember why I'm supposed to be upset. She's here. She's in my arms, and she loves me. That's all that matters.

"Seriously. I shouldn't have run. I should have trusted in you. In us."

"Are you sure? I'll do anything to make this work, but I know how you feel about the hockey life. The travel. The uncertainty. If we do this, it's forever for me. You're my forever." I don't know why I'm reminding her of the downfalls that come with dating a player. Honesty. That's why. If we're going into this thing, we're doing it for real with eyes wide open. Not the rushed secret of our incredible weekend together. This can't be a mistake for her, because it's sure as shit not a mistake for me.

"I know. I know it will be hard, but the thing I didn't consider before was that I'm looking for certainty, right? And you're that for me. You're my constant. The only person in my life that has always been there for me. No matter what. I shouldn't have doubted that. Being a hockey player doesn't turn you into a cheating asshole. It just makes it easier to be one. You're not my dad."

"I sure the fuck hope not, because those would be some pretty unholy thoughts I'd be having about you." Her laugh comes out wet and wobbly.

I swipe my thumbs along her freckled cheeks wiping away the hot tears streaking her face. "Don't cry, baby."

"They're happy tears. I'm happy. I promise."

My lips capture hers again. She's clutching at my cheeks and squirming in my arms when a voice breaks through our heated embrace.

"Um. Maybe we should head home, so you two can finish this."

Jazz is standing next to me looking unimpressed. "Jazz. Hi. Sorry." I give her a sheepish wave.

"It's fine. You're welcome, and I'm happy for you, but let's get out of here." She rattles her keys in my face.

I reluctantly let Jordan slide down my body, keeping a tight hold of her hand. She's stuck with me now. I'm not letting her go. Ever.

# Chapter Thirty

## Jordan

I snuggle into Aspen's side in the back of Mr. Ellory's industrial sized van, curling into his big warm body. It has to be massive to cart his seven children around. They still have three under ten, so random Cheerios litter the seats, and a rainbow hodgepodge of melted crayons lines the cup holders. I like it. It's homey even if the slightly funky smell wrinkles my nose when I first climb in.

"Tough break, son. But you played a fantastic game."

"Thanks, Dad." Aspen is subdued but still smiling after the Lightning lost in the finals of the Frozen Four. "It's ok. Next year is our year. Seb will be back on the ice. Dream team reunited. We can do it." The merest shadow of a doubt crosses behind his eyes. He's worried about Sebastian. They all are. Me too. I love the guys. They're like the long-lost big brothers I never had.

I trace an infinity symbol on his palm while leaning in to drop my head onto his chest. I wish I could have flown out to see him play, but it didn't work out with my exams, and running the store. So, I did the next best thing and watched with his family at their house. It was electric. His younger siblings were so excited watching their big brother on tv. Wait until he's playing for the league.

"Willow, Cedar, and Oak wanted to meet you at the airport, but your dad ixnayed that idea. He thought you might already be overwhelmed."

"I'm glad. I'll be happy to see them, but I needed the drive home to prepare myself. Not to mention the alone time with you." His breath caresses my cheek as he leans in, whispering in my ear.

"Well, kind of alone." I nod my head to his dad in the driver's seat, studiously ignoring us.

Close enough. He squeezes my hand as we pull into the driveway of his family home. The three youngest are all standing on the wooden front porch, waiting to greet Aspen.

"You know. I will never be able to look at Oak without imagining he's the secret heir to fairy."

"Oak? That dork? He's not cool enough to be fae." And that's what I love about Aspen. Well, one of the many things. He might not share my love of all things fantasy, but he knows what I'm talking about.

I snort. "Don't call your brother a dork. That's mean."

"Oh, you would not believe the things that innocent looking jerk has called me."

He pretends to be annoyed, but a warm smile spreads across his face when he's talking about his brother. He's so lucky to have such a big, caring family. A big, caring family that embraced me right along with him. They have seven kids, and over the years they folded me in as if I was their eighth. I'm not sure how I missed it before. They've always been there for me. When Mom wasn't there for me, the Ellorys were there to sub in. They're the family I've been searching for my whole life, not noticing I already had them.

"Hey, wait." He pulls me back to him when I try to slide down the rough velour seat.

His arms swallow me up in a tight hold, and my chest crashes against his as he yanks me into him. My mouth opens under his seeking tongue, and his hands slip up my back, trailing a line of shivery heat before tangling in my hair.

We're desperate, clashing tongues and grasping hands. If this is what reunions are like after time apart, I can live with his travel schedule.

Loud clapping breaks us up, and we collapse against each other, laughing until we're gasping for breath. Right. His entire family is waiting for us, and we were making out in the back seat of his parents' messy van like a couple of horny teenagers.

His touch sends another shiver through me as he brushes my hair behind my ear, leaning in with a whisper. "Don't worry. There's more of that to come later. I've missed you, Jordy." The words are a promise. For today and every day after for the rest of our lives.

# Chapter Thirty-One

## Epilogue

"**B**ring that box of books over here. No, put it there. Has Dev managed to fix the AC? I don't want to sweat Melanie out of the store. She'll never come back."

I place the heavy box on the floor in the second spot she pointed to. She'll change her mind five more times before her author gets here, but I don't care. I'd move them a hundred times for her if that's what she wanted. I reach out and grab her hand as she flies by in a fluttery whirlwind. "Hey, babe." She lets me pull her to my side, and I drop my face into the top of her head. The sweet floral scent of her hairspray invades my senses, and I can't resist taking a deep inhale. "It's gonna be ok."

"But what if..."

"No what ifs. You've planned this perfectly. Every single detail is in order. Check out that line out front? Look how organized it is. That was you, babe." I gently turn her around, so she can see out the glass front window, propping my chin on top of her head.

"I know, but..."

"Nope. You've got this. Look at them. All bought tickets, and all waiting patiently to meet their favorite author. The ecommerce shop has been picking up thanks to your hard work and connections. You're totally boss bitching it."

She spins in my arms. "Thank you, Aspen. For everything. For the support and getting your hockey bros out here to help. Do you really think Dev can fix the AC?"

"Lucy can do anything with his hands." My teammate emerges from the back room a moment later, nodding and swiping at the grease streak on his cheek.

Jordan runs over with a squeal to give him a hug. He freezes, then gives in, wrapping his massive arms around her. Easy boy. I tamp down the jealousy that rears its head when I see her in another man's arms. Not another man. One of my teammates. I trust them both. My Neanderthal brain still wants to lodge a protest, but I shove that idiot back down into his cave.

I wipe the sweat off my brow. Some of the team went home for the summer, but a lot of us are here, enduring the July heat wave. They all came to help Jordan out. She's a member of the family now too. The store looks incredible, all decorated like a fantasy themed forest. Vines trailing from the ceiling, flickering LED lights, mimicking the look of candlelight, and a full moon and starry sky projected on the back wall. They all helped in spite of a few complaints. "I play hockey. I don't decorate shit."

Were Jackson's words, but he said them with his usual smile, and jumped right in, hanging greenery from the walls.

I'm going to miss these guys after I graduate, but I've still got one year left to enjoy this. After that, I'll make a new family. A new team. In a new city. Fingers crossed. Chicago. And with the success Jordan is making of the bookstore, she's already talking about opening a second location wherever we end up. She can hire someone else to manage this place when her mom flakes or maybe completely buy her out.

The possibilities stretching in front of us are endless.

"Don't punch Lucy. You'll mess up that pretty face of his." Sebastian gives me a tentative smile as he slaps me on the back. I'm happy to see him here. He showed up without a complaint. Jordan has that effect on the guys. They'll do anything for her. He's been dragging himself out of his dark place now that they cleared him to start training again. He's still not there, but hopefully soon. With him back on the team, we can win the championship this year. It was a disappointing loss in the finals, but I know we're going to go all the way, and if we do, that'll earn me my spot to play professionally.

Jordan's phone buzzes, and she runs to me, eyes shining. "She's here. Come with me."

My big hands swallow up her cheeks when I cup them, bending my head down to meet her lips. She melts into me for just a moment before shoving me off. "You had better not have wrecked my lipstick, Aspen."

I laugh. "You're perfect."

"Come on. I can't keep her waiting." She drags me to the back door, excitement bubbling over.

I sling an arm over her shoulder as she leans her hip into the crash bar to push the door open, facing the future as a team.

Thanks for reading Aspen and Jordan's story. If you're interested in getting to know the guys of the Lakeview Lightning, Sebastian is up next.

**Meet Abby and Sebastian:**

*He destroyed her trust in high school, and she swore she'd never date a hockey player.*

*But now he's back in her life, and they've both got new scars.*

*They can't seem to stay away from each other.*

*Even when they know, they both might get burned.*

**Devour the next installment of the Lakeview Lightning series. Read The Comeback now.**

# ALSO BY

## The Lakeview Lightning Series

### *The Breakout: Book 0.5*
Three days. Two best friends. One Bed. What could possibly go wrong? When Aspen drives his best friend Jordan to a romance book convention, he's not expecting the storm of the century to trap them in a bed and breakfast on the way home. But what happens when the chill of the snow can't cool the fiery heat between them? Available free when you sign up for my newsletter.

### *The Comeback: Book 1*
In the game of love and hockey, second chances are rare, but Abby and Sebastian are about to get theirs. From childhood friends to heartbreak, their story is a testament to the power of forgiveness, and the courage to face one's fears. Available in ebook and discreet paperback.

### The Red Line: Book 2
The Red Line takes you on a wild ride where hearts and skates collide. Natasha and Jackson's tale is a fiery mix of passion, and ice, challenging the rules of the game and love. Will they be able to keep things hot when their no-strings fling grows into something more? Available in ebook and discreet paperback.

### The Game: Book 3
These two college seniors have some serious ex problems. And fake dating is the perfect solution. But when the steam between them gets too hot, they both might end up getting burned. Available in ebook and discreet paperback.

### The Penalty: Book 4
Don't date his teammates. Cece had no intention of breaking her brother's one rule. Until the weekend that changed everything... This grumpy sunshine brother's best friend story is available in ebook and discreet paperback.

### The Opposition: Book 5
Beau's story, coming 2025.

# About the Author

Nikki Jewell is a steamy romance author from Ontario, Canada. When she's not mainlining caffeine, Nikki loves writing fictional women who bring their men to their knees. Literally and figuratively. When she's not writing, she escapes the confines of her writing cave to wander the great outdoors, communing with trees, birds, and squirrels that judge her for drinking coffee in the wilderness. Nikki's secret identity as a romance writer is so well-guarded that her twin children don't know about her double life. But her husband is the real-life hero who keeps the inspiration flowing, even when her characters refuse to cooperate. He likes to say he's her muse.

You can follow Nikki on Instagram, Threads, and TikTok @nikkijewell_books to keep up with her latest shenanigans.

 instagram.com/nikkijewell_books

 tiktok.com/@nikkijewell_books

Manufactured by Amazon.ca
Bolton, ON